I0690197

Men at Work II

First Edition

Published by The Nazca Plains Corporation
Las Vegas, Nevada
2009

ISBN: 978-1-935509-61-5

Published by

The Nazca Plains Corporation ®
4640 Paradise Rd, Suite 141
Las Vegas NV 89109-8000

PUBLISHER'S NOTE
Men at Work II is a work of fiction created wholly by *Christopher
Trevor*'s imagination. All characters are fictional and any resemblance
to any persons living or deceased is purely by accident. No portion
of this book reflects any real person or events.

Cover Photo, Les Byerley
Art Director, Blake Stephens

Dedication

For the business suited, neck-tied, wingtipped
and high socked men of Wall Street.

Men at Work II

First Edition

Christopher Trevor

Table of Contents

Table of Contents Continued...

Introduction

And here we are again with more of those hardworking men that we respect so much. Greetings once again Constant Readers and a hearty welcome to all new readers of my work. When I had written and put together the stories for my book "Men at Work" I hadn't thought about a second collection of erotic tales so soon. But as the legend goes for some writers the stories do tend to write themselves and in my case I found myself writing more stories about "Men at Work." In this second collection of erotic tales I have chosen to pay homage to hotel bellboys (or bellhops if you prefer), handsome young marines, professional bodybuilders, office and restaurant executives, construction workers, college baseball players and of course when it comes to "Men at Work" no collection would be complete without a cop fetish story. Read what occurs when a bellboy working in a ritzy hotel finds a handsome executive asleep in his room in his business attire minus his dress shoes. Marines are featured in two stories in this book. In the first military tale a young unsuspecting marine finds himself to be the victim of a uniform thief. This tale was written by me and the Webmaster at "Boundguys.com", Catiff himself. In the next military tale Cleeve and Otis make an appearance when they capture and brutally work over a man in uniform. Besides men that must work for a living I have included in this collection a kinky story starring a professional bodybuilder who winds up in heavy bondage and is forced through a harrowing workout by his captors. No book of mine starring "Men at Work" would be complete (at least in my opinion) without at least one or a few tales of handsome executives in and out of their dress socks. In this book my sheer socked buddy Alex is working at an inn as a headwaiter when a patron becomes transfixed with his sheer dress socks and in the story "The Story of Lenny and Frank" two executives discover a mutual foot fetish. Playing hooky does not happen just in school, it also happens to overworked "Men at Work." Read what happens to a hunky executive who decides to take a day off from work at the beach when he encounters some new equally hunky buddies in the story "On the Beach." As most of my readers know from my past works, besides men in uniform and business attire I am also a true fetishist for men in baseball uniforms. In "A Party after the Ball Game" a college baseball player is unwittingly captured and brought to a real kinky party where he finds himself to be the main course of a group of other lusty college dudes. The book winds out with an erotic rubber fetish tale entitled "Rubber Pig." I co-authored this tale with my good buddy "Anonymous Cop." I had never written a rubber fetish story before and I must say I had a ball working on this one with my anonymous cop buddy.

As always, Happy Reading,

-Christopher Trevor-

The Bellboy

My name is Sam. I work as a bellboy in a hotel in New York City. What I want to tell you about happened a few months ago. It was a Wednesday, around six thirty P.M. Mr. Franklin, the hotel manager had summoned me to the front desk.

"You asked to see me Mr. Franklin?" I asked him when I went over to him.

I was dressed in my red bellboy uniform, complete with the pillbox style hat.

"Yes Sam, I need for you to do me a favor," he said to me. "All the maids are busy at the moment and Mr. Williamson in room seven eight seven needs some stuff brought up to his room right away."

That was all Mr. Franklin had to say. Mr. Williamson was a vice president from a bank. He was in New York on a serious business trip, and from what I heard everything the man wanted the man got, right away.

"What does Mr. Williamson need sir?" I asked Mr. Franklin.

"Some fresh towels, bars of soap, shampoo, and a cold bottle of champagne," Mr. Franklin said, reading from a piece of hotel stationery. "Where the champagne is concerned he wants a bottle of our very best."

"I'll get on it now sir," I said to Mr. Franklin, already thinking about the big tip I would receive from the rich bank vice president.

A little while later I arrived at Mr. Williamson's door with the wagon containing the stuff he had ordered. The sign on the doorknob was turned to "Maid, please make up room" so I just figured Mr. Williamson was out somewhere and took out my master key. I opened the door, took the stack of towels off the wagon and walked into the room. As I was walking toward the bathroom with the towels I saw Mr. Williamson. He was stretched out on a recliner; he was easily one of the handsomest men I had laid eyes on in a long time. He had dark hair cut and parted in a corporate style, and he appeared to be pretty tall. He was sleeping on the recliner, snoring softly. He was dressed in a white shirt with the top button undone and his silk tie pulled down, navy blue trousers, and dark blue nylon dress socks. His big feet were propped up on the footrest of the recliner. His wing tip shoes were next to the recliner on the floor and his suit jacket was lying on the nearby couch. My breath caught in my throat as I walked past him with the towels. He looked to be about thirty or thirty-two years old. I put the towels in the bathroom and returned to the wagon to get the soap and shampoo. As I walked past him again Mr. Williamson stirred in his sleep and stretched his legs out in front of himself so that now his big executive feet were dangling off the footrest. My mouth filled with saliva and I swallowed hard. I put the soap and shampoo in the bathroom and went to get the champagne. As I took the champagne off the wagon a sinister thought struck me. Temptation to say the least. With the bottle of champagne in my hand I closed the door to Mr. Williamson's room. I looked at him as I past him to put the bottle in the small refrigerator under the bar.

I could not resist. I put the bottle of champagne in the refrigerator and walked silently over to the sleeping handsome executive bank vice president. I kneeled down at his big socked feet and picked up one of his wingtip shoes. I put the inside of the shoe against my nose and mouth and sniffed heavily. It smelled slightly musty and from foot sweat bank executive foot sweat to be exact. I looked up at Mr. Williamson and my dick grew hard in my uniform pants. I moved closer to his socked feet on my knees. I sniffed each of his big feet a few times, heaven to say the least. I knew that I could get fired for this, but *I had to* take the chance. Fucking bank vice president looked like something right out of GQ magazine, and his feet were beautifully shaped. He had the sexiest arches I had ever seen and the way they were outlined under his thin dress socks made them all the more sexy looking it seemed. This was too good to pass up. I stuck out my tongue and pressed the tip of it against the bottom of Mr. Williamson's right foot. He stirred slightly in his sleep as I ran the tip of my tongue up the bottom of his foot, savoring the taste of his foot sweat on his blue nylon dress sock. I ran the tip of my tongue back down his foot, kissing it a few times on the way down. When Mr. Williamson stirred in his sleep again and smacked his lips together I stopped licking his foot, looking up at him from my position down on my knees. He didn't wake up but a small smile played across his lips. Maybe he was dreaming that his wife was licking his smelly tired feet. I smiled and pressed my tongue again against the bottom of his right foot. Now it tasted of sweat and my saliva. I drooled over his toes and watched as my saliva slid down the bottom of his foot. I quickly lapped up my saliva, licking the bottom of his socked foot again. I could not believe the guy hadn't woken up. I moved to the side of the recliner and pressed my tongue against the top of Mr. Williamson's right foot. I licked the top of his foot a few times and kissed it. Looking at the side of his foot I was enraptured by the shape of his ankle through his thin dress sock. As I said he had beautiful arches. His ankles were beautiful as well. I then took the bottom of his pants leg in my fingertips and pulled it up slowly, wondering just how high his socks went. I pulled his pants leg up past his calf and saw that his socks were definitely knee-length. So many executives nowadays opt for that OTC (over the calf) look when it comes to their dress socks. Pure bliss took over me as I let go of his pants leg and went back to licking his sock, resuming at the top of his foot. As I licked his foot though Mr. Williamson began to slowly wake up. When he opened his eyes I was too enthralled in licking his smelly executive sock to notice.

"Mmm…" he crooned as he awoke.

When he saw me and saw what I was doing he nearly bolted off the recliner.

"Mmm…H-hey!!!" Mr. Williamson blurted in shock. "Wh-what are you doing???"

I grabbed his right foot in my hands and looked up at him in fear.

"Y-you were fucking licking my feet!!" he seethed at me. "Holy shit man, fucking bellboy, or bellhop, or whatever it is they call you guys nowadays, you were licking my goddamned feet!"

"Y-yes sir Mr. Williamson, I was," I stammered nervously and gave his big toe a kiss.

"Holy fucking shit!!" he yelled. "What are you, some kind of pervert or something? My damned feet stink. I can smell that pungency from my socks from here. I've been wearing those damned socks since six AM and you're licking them as if they tasted like ice cream or something!"

Shaking nervously I leaned forward and still holding Mr. Williamson's foot in my hands I gave his big toe a few sucks through his blue nylon sock. I wanted to show him how the pungency and aroma emanating from his socks was not all that bad to me, actually it was heaven he had in those socks of his. He leaned forward, watching me intently.

"Shit, now you're sucking my toe as if it was a dick," he said. "But I have to admit that does feel sort of nice."

"Sit back and relax Mr. Williamson," I said without looking up at him. "Sit back and allow me to service your big executive feet."

"I don't know about this guy," he said, sounding uncertain. "I mean, I've never had anyone lick my feet before."

"I promise you won't regret it," I said to him and kissed the bottom of his foot a few times.

He seemed to mull it over for a few seconds, trying to act as if he were not enjoying what I was doing at that moment.

"Okay guy, go for it," Mr. Williamson said, acting like he had just made a big executive decision. "And when you're done cleaning my socks you'll service my smelly feet, bare."

"Yes sir," I said as he leaned back in the recliner.

I resumed licking his right foot, inwardly looking forward to getting to his left foot and then his bare feet.

"I don't believe this, fucking guy is licking my raunchy feet," Mr. Williamson said with a smile of disbelief on his face.

I licked, sucked, and kissed Mr. Williamson's smelly feet, drooling over them, and licking up my saliva off his socks. He hiked his pants legs up to his knees, letting me service his socks all the way up. I licked them like my life depended on it and slowly worked my way back down to the bottoms of his feet.

"You really like licking my big smelly executive feet huh guy?" he asked me.

"Yes sir, I do," I replied and licked greedily at the bottoms of his feet.

"Do those long executive socks of mine taste good?" he asked me mockingly.

"Yes sir, they do," I said.

I wrapped my fingers around his beautiful ankles and licked the tops of his feet over and over again, sniffing in the aroma of his foot sweat at the same time.

"What's your name guy?" he asked me.

"Sam sir, my name is Sam," I replied.

"Well Sam, I have a feeling that you and I are going to be friends, good friends," Mr. Williamson said as he pulled off his tie, undoing the knot in it as he went along.

"I hope so sir, I certainly hope so," I replied in between licking his socks.

Holding him tightly by his ankles I kissed Mr. Williamson's feet all over and then up to his knees, drooling over his socks as I went along and licking up my saliva.

"Yeah Sam, we're going to be real good friends," Mr. Williamson murmured as he unbuttoned his crisp white shirt.

I looked up and saw him taking off his shirt.

"Keep licking my socks Sam, don't stop," he said. "Man, *that feels good.*"

He tossed his shirt and tie aside and leaned back in the recliner again, his hands up behind his head. His body was like a rock. It looked like he spent a good amount of time at the gym. His biceps were the size of bowling balls. His shoulders were wide as a doorway. His stomach region was washboard flat and his robust chest was hairy and adorned with silver dollar sized nipples, all day suckers I call nipples like that.

"Yeah Sam, keep licking those socks of mine," he said breathlessly.

A little while later Mr. Williamson told me to stop licking his feet, only temporarily. He ordered me to go and get the bottle of champagne from out of the refrigerator. As I walked over to the bar he quickly pulled his suit pants off himself and tossed them on the couch. As I took the bottle out of the refrigerator Mr. Williamson took his socks off and put them back on again, inside out.

"Ahhhh, there you go Sam, a real treat for you now," he said, leaning back in the recliner with his feet propped on the footrest. "I'll bet the insides of my socks will taste even better than the outsides did. Now, pour me some champagne and then you can get back to work on my feet."

Minutes later, with a glass of champagne in his hand Mr. Williamson watched as I resumed licking his feet. He sat there in just his white briefs and blue socks.

"Taste good Sam?" he asked me and sipped his champagne.

"Yes sir," I replied as the raunchy smell of the insides of his socks assaulted my nose. "*Phewww…*"

"Yeah, just like I said Sam, a real treat for you," Mr. Williamson said mockingly.

He sipped the champagne as I licked the arches of his big sexy feet.

"Ahhhh yeah, this hotel sure does provide good service," Mr. Williamson said.

Ten minutes or so past and I was still licking and kissing Mr. Williamson's socked feet.

"Say Sam, you must be getting thirsty after all this," Mr. Williamson said to me. "Would you like some champagne?"

"Oh yes Sir Mr. Williamson, I would love a drink of something cold at this point," I replied gratefully and kissed his socked toes a few times.

"Okay, pour some of that champagne over my socks and lap it up," he ordered.

I did as he told me and soaked both his socked feet with the champagne. He watched with satisfaction as I resumed licking his feet, sucking up the champagne at the same time. As I licked and sucked his socks the phone on the table next to the recliner rang. I didn't even pause as he answered it.

"Hello?" Mr. Williamson said into the receiver. "Oh, hi Steve, how are you?"

He paused to listen to Steve's response.

"I'm fine buddy, and the meeting went great, just great," Mr. Williamson said and paused to listen again. "What am I doing now? You would not believe me if I told you bud."

Mr. Williamson looked down at me and smiled.

"Well, after the meeting in the hotel conference room I came back up here and ordered some stuff sent up to my room," he said into the receiver. "Then I shucked off my suit jacket and shoes and being that I had been up real early I conked out in a recliner. When I woke up there was this bellboy here and the fucking guy was licking my socked feet."

Mr. Williamson paused again and smiled wickedly as he listened to whatever Steve was saying. Judging from the smile on Mr. Williamson's face Steve did not or could not believe what he had just heard.

"Yes you heard me correctly Steve, the bellboy was licking my damned stinking socked feet," Mr. Williamson repeated into the receiver. "Matter of fact he's still here *and he's still at it.* I turned my smelly socks inside out on my feet and he *still* went on licking them. Fucking guy loves my damned smelly executive feet."

Another pause as Mr. Williamson listened.

"Yeah I know how bad my feet stink at the end of the day Steve, but this bellboy is truly loving every second of licking my damned feet," he went on happily. "And I have to admit it feels so fucking good I don't want the guy to stop. Listen, I made him pour champagne over my socks and now he's busy sucking it all out of them."

I had to wonder how whoever Steve was knew that Mr. Williamson's feet stunk at the end of the day.

Mr. Williamson looked down at me again and said that his buddy Steve could not believe what he was telling him. After a few more minutes of talking business on the phone with Steve Mr. Williamson hung up and looked at me with a smile.

"You really are something Sam," he said to me. "Just look at you, sitting there like an obedient puppy, licking my damned feet."

When I was done sucking the champagne out of Mr. Williamson's socks my head was sort of spinning. I watched as he rolled his socks off his feet and laid his now big bare feet on the footrest of the recliner.

"Okay Sam, now for the real treat," Mr. Williamson said, wiggling his toes. "Lick my bare smelly feet till they're clean as a whistle and smelling fresh as daisies."

I immediately got to work, starting at the bottom of his right foot. His bare feet tasted raunchy, musty, and cheesy, just the way I love them. I licked in between all his toes and sucked those toes like crazy.

"Damn, no one would believe this shit," he murmured contentedly.

When I returned to the front desk Mr. Franklin asked what had taken me so long. I told him that I had run into a distraction in Mr. Williamson's room but that I had taken care of it, adding that everything was fine now. Smiling, I squeezed the blue nylon executive dress socks that were in my pocket, a souvenir, given to me by the handsome Mr. Williamson.

/The End/

Grunt

Written by: Catiff and Christopher Trevor

Corporal Lewis was in trouble. No, that was putting it mildly. The handsome brown haired corporal was in a shit-load of trouble. During his leave time from the marines, on his vacation he had gone out to the bars in uniform. He was thinking that all decked out and spiffy in his uniform it would get him girls. Instead it had made him a target for some psychotic dude who had decided to get the drop on the man in uniform. Drunk as a skunk and none too bright at the moment Lewis had gone out to piss in an alley behind one of the bars because the bathroom was crowded and disgusting. The corporal did not relish the thought of his marine issued shoes stomping around in other men's piss on the bathroom floor of the bar.

Lewis had barely managed to pull his dick out to piss before he felt the butt of a pistol smash into the back of his head. His uniform cap hat took a lot of the blow, but everything exploded white, the corporal saw his hat go flying and then everything went black. As he lay there on the ground unconscious the man who had smashed him with the gun butt chuckled as the marine's cock let loose a torrent of piss all over the ground in front of him where he lay. When the marine was done pissing the man gently stuffed his pride and joy back into his olive colored uniform trousers. When he was done the kidnapper licked his fingers, relishing the taste of the marine's manhood that lingered there.

When Lewis came to the first thing he noticed was that it was completely dark. The back of his head ached miserably. The second thing the corporal noticed was that when he tried to move around his hands were tied tightly behind his back. Lewis had no idea what was going on. He could feel himself moving and the sounds of an engine. He also detected an odor of gas. My God, he realized, he was in the trunk of a car. He had been kidnapped somehow, a marine's worst nightmare made real. He thought about screaming out for help and perhaps kicking his feet against the trunk. But he quickly decided against those things, seeing as he did not know where he was, if there was anyone around who could come to his aid and what he might suffer in retaliation if he did try to attract unwanted attention.

When the car stopped and he heard the driver get out and open the trunk Lewis still could not see. He realized then that he was not only tied up but blindfolded as well.

"Listen, whoever you are, I don't know who you are or what this is all about but you don't fuck with a marine!" Lewis shouted.

The only response he received was a punch to the gut.

"HOOOOOFFF!!!" the marine sputtered.

Lewis was pulled out of the trunk of the car and marched with his hands tied behind him, a length of rope tied over his upper torso pinning his arms to his sides and blindfolded into what he assumed was the basement of a house. He felt hands guiding him by his upper arms down a flight of stairs. Having regained some air Lewis tried yelling for help but a hand was clasped quickly and tightly over his mouth. Now the marine could only moan helplessly. Lewis continued struggling, hoping to get free but it was no use it seemed. The ropes were tied too tight. Once at the bottom of the stairs the marine's kidnapper, losing patience gave his captive another hard punch to the gut.

"HOOOFFFFF!!!" Lewis sputtered a second time and collapsed to his knees, gasping for air.

But this time he was not given time to recover as a knee connected with his chin.

"ARRRHHHHH!!!" the marine yelped miserably.

"Don't think that just because I haven't killed you that I won't change my mind Soldier boy," Lewis heard a male voice say, sounding harsh.

"Fuck you man, I'm no soldier boy, I'm a marine and..." Lewis began but for his rant he received yet another knee to the chin. "ARRRHHHHHH!!! Fucker!!!"

"Marine, yeah, all the more reason I'm going to have some fun with you," the guy said, sounding psychotic now. "Do what I say man, or else! You understand?"

Lewis could only grunt his compliance. Being gut punched and kneed to the chin had shaken him. He barely put up a struggle as a foul tasting rag was pulled tightly between his teeth and tied around his head. The kidnapper seemed to be taking pleasure in roughing Lewis up as he gagged him.

"Ha, I used this gag on the last man in uniform I had here Soldier boy," the kidnapper laughed. "What you're tasting is his saliva and spit all over it...HA!!"

Lewis could feel the rag bight into the sides of his mouth as his captor tied it securely and cruelly tight. And what was that the guy had said about the gag having been used on the last man in uniform he had here??? What was this that Lewis had been thrust into he thought miserably. The marine let out a small moan, half pain and half anger in protest.

"Oh you like that Sunshine?" his captor asked mockingly. "Because I have more. I am going to make sure that that pretty mouth of yours is well gagged. I don't want to hear you whining when I start giving you orders.'

Lewis most definitely did not like the sound of that. He heard what sounded like tape being pulled off a roll and sure enough, the marine found his mouth being sealed shut. Awful of awfuls Lewis thought, now the rag was jammed in his mouth and every time he swallowed he would taste whoever's saliva it was on the rag. The guy had said it had been used to gag another man in uniform. Lewis thought miserably if the man in uniform before him had also been a marine trapped here. The marine then could feel his feet being pushed together and tightly bound.

"Okay Princess, you stay here and get comfortable," Lewis heard the guy say.

Princess??? Sunshine??? Somehow Lewis liked being called Soldier boy a lot more now.

"You're going to be tied up and gagged for a long while," the kidnapper went on and Lewis' skin crawled. "You may as well get used to it. And don't try making any noise. I gagged you for a reason. You'll have plenty to cry about when the fun starts, trust me on that Soldier boy."

"MMMFFFFF!!!" Lewis moaned and received a smack on the head.

Cowed now, he stayed silent. Only when he heard no more movement and was sure he was alone did he try to move. Lewis struggled against the ropes that bound his hands, chest and feet but they were mercilessly tight. The more he struggled the tighter his bonds seemed to get, if that were possible. The marine had no way of knowing how much time had passed when he finally stopped squirming and struggling. Blindfolded, the world was only a hazy blur of light and shadows that intruded under the bandanna covering his eyes.

Finally fatigued and hung over from all the drinks he had consumed earlier that evening Lewis gave up all his struggles. He rolled about for a while, hoping perhaps to find a way to get comfortable in his bondage. Eventually the marine thought he fell asleep.

He could not tell if he was dreaming at first. The sensory deprivation screwed with his mind. His head was filled with weird sensations, not to mention his head still smarted from having been pistol whipped earlier. The poor marine could not even tell when he was awake or asleep. But Lewis then felt his body being lifted up and his hands untied. Was he being rescued???

"Okay Petunia, rise and shine, the funs about to begin," Lewis heard the kidnapper say and his heart sunk like the Titanic.

"Petunia???" Lewis said to himself. "Fucking Petunia???"

Grunt (Part 2)

Written by: Catiff and Christopher Trevor

Corporal Lewis was soon completely untied and just as the last of the ropes were undone from his feet he decided he would pounce and really teach this fucker who had so brazenly kidnapped him a lesson. The well-trained marine figured he would simply whip the blindfold off and pummel the guy. The gag, er- the gags would come off after he was done teaching whoever this dude was a lesson. Inwardly Lewis had hoped against hope that all this had been a sick and twisted joke played on him by some of his buddies in the service with him. But being pistol whipped over the head back in that alley was not a joke his buddies would have played on him. No, all of this was too real the young marine realized more and more.

Once the ropes were off his feet the kidnapper kept Lewis gagged and blindfolded as he helped him to his feet to a standing position.

"MMMFFFFF!!!" Lewis sputtered angrily and pulled out of the man's grasp, thinking, "I'm not tied up now fucker!!"

But just as Lewis was about to, as he had thought, pummel the guy, the marine heard the click of a gun.

"It's pointing right at that nice muscular chest of yours Soldier boy," Lewis heard the guy say. "To be honest I don't want to bloody up that pretty uniform of yours, but if I have to I will."

The marine, terror stricken, froze in place and without thinking raised his hands high...

He whimpered miserably as he heard the kidnapper chuckle.

"RHUUUU ru ahnt?" Lewis blubbered through his gag, trying to say, "What do you want?"

"HA, that's rich, trying to talk through two gags Soldier boy," the guy laughed and Lewis heard the gun click again.

The marine shivered in his shoes and socks.

"Trying to talk when I didn't even give you permission to do so," the guy said, sounding more and more psychotic now. "But I can understand your confusion over all of this, so this one time I will forgive you. As for what I want, ah, that is a good question and you are about to find out my pet. Because what I want is what you're presently wearing, your uniform.

"Rhy rhuniforn? Rar rhu rout ruv rhur ruckin' nine?" Lewis gurgled, clenching his raised hands into fists, trying to say, "My uniform? Are you out of your fucking mind?"

The man simply chuckled in response. Lewis wanted to tell him that there was no way he was taking his uniform off, but seeing as he was still helplessly in this man's power he really didn't see any way out of it.

"Now, I suppose there are a few ways we can go about this Soldier boy," the man said and again Lewis heard the click of the gun.

The marine's breath caught in his throat...

"I want you to do it blindfolded for me, somehow watching you strip out of your uniform that way will be very tantalizing, wouldn't you agree?" the man asked the captive marine in a mocking manner. "Putting a bullet in you really is the last thing I want to do, but as I said, if I have to I will. Another way to get you stripped is I can again bash you over the head with this gun and then strip you myself. Yes, that actually might be fun, handling that hard marine body of yours while I remove all your clothes. Just like it felt so good when I knocked you out in that alley and carried you over my shoulder to my car, HA! I had you slung over my shoulder like a side of beef and one hand over that sweet tight ass of yours. Now, it's all up to you my pet, which way do you want to do this?"

Lewis wanted to be able to say: "Fuck you, I'm not your pet you fucking asshole," but he thought better of it and slowly lowered his arms. The marine began by unbuttoning his uniform jacket. He shucked it down his muscular arms and let it drop to the floor beside him. Very unbecoming for a marine he thought, dropping his pride and joy uniform to the floor.

"That's it Soldier boy, do it in sections," the guy said, now sounding scarily reasonable.

"Ruckin' rervert," Lewis muttered, trying to say, "Fucking pervert."

Obviously the marine was wondering miserably why he had been kidnapped just so he could be made to do a striptease for whoever the fuck this guy was.

Next he undid the knot in his tie, dropped it to the floor and began unbuttoning his shirt. He heard the kidnapper taking deep breaths as he bared his muscular hairy chest.

"Fuck, the marines really do a job on getting you grunts in shape huh Soldier boy?" the kidnapper said.

Lewis found himself nodding "Yes" and placed his hands over his stomach before taking his unbuttoned shirt off.

The guy brazenly gave one of the marine's big pink nipples a fast squeeze followed by a bottle-cap twist.

"MMMMFFF..." Lewis moaned and unhitched his uniform trousers.

He felt an overwhelming sense of humiliation as he slid his uniform trousers down his legs and off. Needless to say he nearly tripped and nearly lost his balance a few times as he de-panted himself. Stripping down while blindfolded was not an easy task the captive marine realized.

"Very nice Soldier boy, very nice indeed," Lewis heard the guy say as he now stood there in just a pair of gray boxer shorts and calf length black cotton socks.

Lewis wanted to ask the guy if he was some kind of crazy voyeur. He wondered if looking at the marine in his underpants and socks was giving him a cheap thrill of some kind. Fuck, kidnapping a marine was not only a shitty ass thing to do to him, but it was against the law as well Lewis was thinking with his tortured mind. But forcing him to strip out of his uniform, his pride and joy was beyond mortifying.

"Okay, now, back on the floor and hands behind you Soldier boy," Lewis heard the kidnapper say and he groaned awfully as he felt his hands being retied once more behind him.

He sat there in his boxer shorts and socks, de-uniformed and feeling totally embarrassed, more embarrassed than he had ever felt in his life. Being captured like this was humiliating enough, he was just a marine out that night on the prowl for some beautiful women, but being forced to strip out of his uniform was beyond humiliating He would rather have stripped for a couple of pretty ladies.

The marine sat with his legs crossed in front of him feeling awful and appalled as the guy, whoever the hell he was bound up his hands behind him again. Looking the scantily clad marine over the kidnapper liked what he saw. He had to chuckle aloud when he saw the beginnings of an erection tenting the front of his captive's boxer shorts.

"Hmm, somehow I'm getting the feeling that you're enjoying all this huh Soldier boy?" the guy asked with a feeling of elation and an erection of his own in his pants.

Lewis nodded his head "No" furiously from side to side as his hands were done being bound behind him.

"That's a good chowder head," the guy laughed, tagging Lewis with yet another offensive sounding nickname. "See? If you cooperate nothing bad will happen to you. Well, maybe that's not one hundred percent correct, but trust me, it is far better that you cooperate because the punishments that I can administer can be far, far worse if you don't."

The guy stepped to the front of the seated marine and told him to stretch his legs out in front of him. With no choice whatsoever in the matter Corporal Lewis did as he was told.

"Here, let me get your socks off for you, I'll be needing them as well as the rest of your uniform Soldier boy," the kidnapper said and peeled Lewis' moist and funky scented black cotton socks from his feet.

Clad now in just his boxer shorts Lewis felt just about totally put on display. He wondered if the guy would help himself to his underpants as well, JEEZ!

"Now, I've always wanted to be a man in uniform," Lewis heard his captor say as the guy got busy retying his bared feet. "Now here is my chance huh Chowder head?"

The marine simply stared in blindfolded darkness at the direction the voice was coming from. He then sensed his pile of clothing being picked up. What did this fucking weird and sick guy mean that he had always wanted to be a man in uniform??? What in all hell was going on here??? The marine squirmed and seethed in his bondage as the sounds of someone getting undressed filled the room…

Grunt (Part 3)

Written by: Catiff and Christopher Trevor

As captured marine Corporal Lewis squirmed around on the floor in bondage, wearing only his boxer shorts, a blindfold and two gags he listened for the sounds of his captor. The marine heard a pair of shoes clonking to the floor followed by the sounds of pants being unhitched and then slid down a pair of legs. What in all hell was this about? He had been captured in an alley when he'd gone to take a piss, brought blindfolded and bound to an unknown destination and then forced to strip at gunpoint out of his uniform *while blindfolded.* Now he heard the man who had captured him getting undressed himself. Was he planning perhaps to rape the marine Corporal Lewis wondered in fear. If that was the case and he was feeling fear why in all hell was his cock rock hard in his boxer shorts then???

Unknown to the squirming and bound up, gagged and blindfolded marine the man who had captured him was indeed removing his own clothing. He stripped down to his underpants and then looked over at the tied up marine, his exceptionally well-toned body as he pulled on the corporal's black socks. The man's dick throbbed in his underpants as he next helped himself to the marine's uniform trousers.

A short while later Corporal Lewis, straightened up into a seated position on the floor once more felt the man hunkered down beside him.

"You ready for this Soldier boy? You ready to see what I've wrought tonight my chowder head?" the kidnapper asked, his fingers toying meanly with the side of Lewis' blindfold.

"MMMFFF…" was Lewis' reply.

"Perfect, this is all so very perfect," the kidnapper said breathlessly and placed a hand over Lewis' blindfold, pushing it up slowly till it became a regular bandanna tied around the corporal's head.

When Lewis' eyes adjusted back to the light of the room he saw first that he was indeed in a basement of some kind. The next thing he took in the sight of caused his eyes to open wide in total shock. His captor, the man who had so brazenly managed to capture him was wearing his uniform.

"MMMMFFFFFF!!!" Corporal Lewis sputtered madly, seeing this guy, who was the same size and build of him wearing his uniform.

It was a disgrace to put it plainly. He had earned the right to wear that uniform. He had suffered through hours upon hours and months and months of PT training to earn the right to wear that uniform. Now this grinning psycho was wearing it and he was wearing nothing more than his underpants. The fucker had even taken his damned socks for crying out loud.

"Har, Har, Har, and har for you my chowder head," the kidnapper chuckled as Lewis stared at him in fear and awe.

With the right haircut this guy could actually pose as him Lewis thought, the possibility of it was enormously frightening. The guy was still hunkered down next to the captured marine, one hand resting gently on his shoulder the other toying with the marine's nipple, squeezing it between his fingers, mashing it, twisting it.

"Hmm, bet you're wondering why in hell I'm all dudied up in your pretty uniform huh Soldier boy?" the kidnapper asked with a grin.

"MMMMMFFFF…" Corporal Lewis groaned chills coursing through him as the man toyed with his nipple.

"Our roles have just been reversed here tonight Chowder head, fuckin' soldier boy," the guy mused with a sinister looking glint in his eyes. "When I saw you at the bar tonight it could not have been more perfect. I know all about the secret project called "The Red Raven" that the military is working on."

At the mention of "The Red Raven" Corporal Lewis' eyes opened wider yet. How had this guy, a goddamned civilian learned of that very secret, very top secret project???

"Dressed in your uniform and with your haircut that I intend to get first thing tomorrow and with your military ID I will be able to infiltrate any military base and learn all I need to know about "Red Raven," Lewis' captor said and finally let go of the corporal's nipple. "Once I've obtained the information from a military computer I'll be able to sell it to the highest bidder."

Lewis watched, sitting there tightly tied as the man stood up and stepped to the stairs that led out of the basement.

"As for you my handsome corporal, that is a whole other story I'm sure," the man said. "Because once I've sold that information I'm sure the military will issue a court martial order for you… Hmm, maybe after all this is done I should sell you to the highest bidder as well…"

"RRRRMMMFFFFFF!!!" Lewis screamed into his gag and then watched forlornly as the man made his way up the steps and out of the basement.

The sound of the door to the basement closing and locking filled the captured marine with a dread he never knew before...

The End/???

A Real Bodybuilding Competition Starring "Hard Pack"

"Fuckers, *slobs,*" the built bigger than big bodybuilder ranted angrily as we pulled and yanked him meanly along by the chains we'd snagged him in. "Bastards, fucking kidnappers, *get these fucking chains off me and then we'll see just how mighty you mugs really are!*"

He was still all sweaty and stinky from having been caught in the sauna and having just competed in a more than hour-long heavy-duty weight lifting competition. He struggled like a madman with his wrists locked in the heavy-duty metal manacles in front of him and hooked up to the chains we'd wound around his muscular forty-six inch chest. We yanked and pulled on the chains on his upper arms, hustling him back up to the gym. The same gym where he'd less than an hour ago was put through and won one of the headiest weight lifting competitions of his career. Steve "Hard Pack" Michaels, fucking weight lifting champion of our district had been snagged by us three more than mean jokers, right out of the sauna he'd been relaxing and dozing in before his appointment with his massage therapist. (An appointment which obviously had been canceled, courtesy of us.) Fucking guy is built bigger than Hercules all six feet two inches of him is sheer hard fucking muscle upon muscle. Man, did we have to work hard to get him chained up back in the sauna. He earned his nickname of "Hard Pack" for a couple of reasons, or so we had heard through the grapevine as it's said. First, because that's just what his muscular body is a fucking hard pack. Second, according to rumor the guy is always sporting a hard pack between his legs. Fuck it all, *I* noticed the hard pack impression in his trademark purple bikini during the weight lifting competition. When asked on the sly about this the guy simply says that hefting weights gets him hard…everywhere. He's won more weight lifting competitions than any of us could remember. We had followed his career for the last ten years or so. According to his personal history he had joined the marines when he was nineteen years old and started weight training way back then, quickly building himself up to the muscle bound Adonis that he now was. He was honorably discharged from the marines at the age of twenty-four, all two hundred and somewhat pounds of sheer muscle of him. He embarked on a fitness career and became one of the top champions in the district. And we always placed our bets on the guy, *always man!* Being that the smooth blond bastard had just won a competition the day before this one we figured we'd bet against him this time out. We figured he'd be too worked over and too tired to win this one. We figured wrong. Fuck, the guys who had run yesterdays competition made "Hard Pack" really fucking sweat bud. I could see the bulges *in their* shorts every time they added weight to the bar he was hefting. I truly got the feeling that they would have really enjoyed working the big fuck over privately in a mean way, just as we were about to do. Fuck, for whatever the reason it really gives some guys a boner to force a big guy like "Hard Pack" through a torturous exercise regime. Another reason we had bet against the "Hard Pack" was that he was competing against a good buddy of ours this time out. It would have been really awesome to see our buddy, a new comer in the competitions win for a change, rather than this muscle bound thirty year old hunk of beef. The poor fuck was now naked as the day he was born, seeing as my buddy Ronald had relieved him of his tight fitting purple Speedo bikini back in the sauna. Fucking guy always wears nothing more than that damned bikini and a pair of white sweat socks tucked down into his marine issued combat boots for the competitions. Well, for this competition he was totally stripped down. (Actually, his bikini was hanging out of the back pocket of Ronald's jeans, Ronald's booby prize for this little escapade.) The bodybuilder's big dick was rage hard in fear, frustration and anger, pointing straight out and his big blond fuzzed balls hung down real low, the size of two kiwis between his muscular tree-trunk like legs. As I said, the guy was always sporting a "hard Pack" between his legs. And at the moment the fact that he was hard and dripping pre cum and piss was pretty awesome let me tell you, seeing as we had playfully jacked the guy off and made him piss good and hard back in the sauna. Well, being that he had consumed a couple of big bottles of mineral water I got the feeling the muscle bound hunk would be pissing more than a good share. Not that we would allow him to use a bathroom mind you. Ha! Built like a mountain and strong as an ox the guy plodded along on his big bare feet as we pulled him slowly along with us.

"Come on Hard Pack, come on bud, you have an appointment for another competition," I said to him snidely, pulling on one of the chains wound around his upper and overly muscular biceps as we struggled to get him into the gym. "Although there's no audience and no one competing against you this time out bud, just you and us three."

"Ha, it would be fun though to have an audience see what the fuck we're going to do to Hard Pack here don't you think man?" my buddy Alex asked laughingly.

"Fucking bastards," Hard Pack grunted, ranted and as he struggled, the chains wrapped tightly around him jangled.

My buddy Alex was pulling the guy along by the chain wound around his other arm. And from behind Ronald was helping to move the big guy along on his bare and stinking feet by pushing and shoving at his sexy muscular ass cheeks. Actually, I think Ronald was having the thrill of his life having those ass cheeks of Hard Pack's cupped and held firmly in his hands. When the muscle fuck really gave us a hard time Ronald would simply jam a finger or two up into the guy's grungy and stinking hole. I think that was another reason that Ronald had relieved "Hard Pack" of his bikini. He wanted easy access to the guy's shit chute. Every time Ronald jammed a finger or two into his hole "Hard Pack" swore like a captured marine, but nonetheless moved along as we wanted him to...

"Almost there now," I teased him as we neared the door to the gym. "You ready for a competition that's going to make you crazy Hard Pack?"

The guy simply glared at me, death in his sheer blue eyes...

"Come on you muscle bound shit head, you don't want to make us have to carry you again now do you?" I teased him meanly.

"Fucking guys, fucking jokers," he snarled. "Bet you mugs thought that was real funny before, picking me up the way you did and carrying my ass from the sauna."

He had been relaxing and dozing in the sauna, as I said earlier when we'd managed to capture him. The chains we'd snagged him in had been in my locker. Oh yes, we had all this planned out way ahead of time. If he won against our good buddy in the competition we had decided that we would make the guy's life more than miserable. And with what we had planned for him miserable was putting it lightly. After he'd won the competition Alex, Ronald and I all looked at each other knowingly while the crowd gathered at the gym applauded the blond hunk yet again... Fuck, I think that even if he lost we would have wanted to capture him. Ha! Fucking guy was as handsome as Adonis and it would be anyone's sadistic pleasure to really work him over in a real nasty and fucked up way. Our buddy who'd lost shook hands with him like a true gentleman and all the blond hunk could meanly say was "Better luck next time Sport." At those words his fate was sealed... We purposely lagged behind in the gym knowing that the guy always relaxed in the sauna after a competition.

"Okay, we're only going to get one chance at this," I said as we quietly took the chains and wrist manacles

from the gym bag in my locker in the lower floor of the gym. "So, we have to do it right the first time... Hard Pack is big enough to take all of us with one hand."

"Got it man," Alex said, holding up the wrist manacles. "Once we got his wrists locked in these he's ours."

The gym had closed and everyone had left except for "Hard Pack" in the sauna and just us three there. The big hunk was friendly with the gym owner so he allowed "Hard Pack" his time in the sauna, provided he locked up the place when he was done cooking himself in there. Luckily for us no one had checked the locker room to make sure anyone was still there... Stealthily we made our way to the sauna...

When we got to the door of the highly heated sauna Alex looked in first. He reported that the big hunk was seated on the top tier, his eyes closed and looking all exhausted and real sweaty.

"Let's do it," Ronald said anxiously but softly. "And I get that damned bikini he's got on."

"Deal," I whispered.

Alex pulled the sauna door open and we crept in. The guy was clad in just his purple trademark bikini, his boots and socks on the floor of the sauna along with three empty quart-sized mineral water bottles. Fuck, the guy was piss hard in his bikini. Alex and I sidled up to the top tier and sat down at the hunk's sides as he dozed, snoring softly…

"Hey Hard Pack," I whispered directly in his ear and with two hands began massaging his upper arm, it felt like concrete.

"Mmmmm…" the bodybuilder crooned as Alex sat next to him at his other side, the wrist manacles at the ready. "I didn't expect you to be massaging me so early Pete. What brings you here already?"

The fucking guy thought I was his massage therapist. I stifled a mean chuckle and prayed that he kept his eyes closed long enough for us to get his wrists locked in the manacles. I worked my hands down his muscular arm to his wrist. Our hearts were pounding as I moved his wrists close together, kneading them as I did so, making the guy think he was getting a preview of his massage.

"Mmmmmm…in a way I'm glad you're here early Pete," Hard Pack said, breathing heavily, his muscular torso glistening with sweat. "I'm goin' to shoot my load like a banshee when you really massage me later man. Fuck, every time I win a competition it puts me in a lather."

We all looked at each other with mean grins on our faces.

"Fuck, when I cum I'm goin' to fill this bikini of mine to capacity," Hard Pack crooned. "And then some."

Then, holding "Hard Pack's" wrists close enough together I nodded at Alex. With his hands slightly trembling he got the manacles positioned over the bodybuilder's wrists. I lifted his wrists just enough and then…the sound of the manacles being snapped and locked shut…

"Gotcha!!" Alex and I shouted delightedly in unison.

"Eh, huh?" Hard Pack said stupidly and opened his eyes, holding up his now trapped wrists, looking at them with stupid wonderment. *"Wh-what the fuck is this???* H-hey, who the fuck are you mugs?"

As he spoke in utter confusion Alex and I were already working at getting the chains wrapped tightly and tied around his upper body, pinning his arms tightly against him.

"Sh-shit, *wh-what the fuck is this all about???"* the heat dazed bodybuilder grunted.

"Just let my boys do their work Hard Pack," Ronald said, standing on the floor facing the guy, reaching for his trademark purple Speedo bikini.

"Y-you guys, I-I saw you upstairs watching the competition," Hard Pack seethed angrily as we chained him tighter and tighter, wrapping his massive bulk in the clanking chains, starting to sweat ourselves in the very heated sauna.

We were all clad in shorts, tee shirts and sneakers but we were sweating nonetheless.

"Yeah, and now you're about to star in a competition all your own Hard Pack," Ronald said gleefully and grabbed a handful of the front of the bodybuilder's purple bikini, giving the enclosed merchandise a mean hard squeeze.

"Ayyyyyyrrrrr GAWD," Hard Pack grunted and arched his body forward in pain as Ronald pulled and slowly got the bikini off the guy. "H-hey man, wh-what do you think you're doing, stealing my damned Speedo!"

"It's my Speedo now," Ronald said and heartily sniffed the crotch area of the bikini a few times. "Mmmmm, smells like a ripe bodybuilder. Tell me Hard Pack, how many times have you filled this teeny weeny bikini with your bodybuilder jazz?"

At that remark we all laughed.

"Shit man, d-don't be stealing my trademark bikini," Hard Pack grunted, his dick hanging real beefy and semi hard over his blond fuzzed balls.

Alex and I could not resist stealing a feel each of his manhood and balls.

"Faggots," the guy seethed as we handled his privates. "One of you better explain all this shit to me, and real fast..."

Once enough length of chain had been secured around Hard Pack's upper torso Alex and I got the short slack of it hooked up to the short chain on his wrist manacles. His entire upper body was now totally immobilized, but with his hands trapped in front of him he would do our bidding.

"Well you see Hard Pack we always bet on you in the competitions," Ronald explained as Alex and I began winding chains around the bodybuilder's upper arms to be used to pull him along with.

"Geez, that's real flattering to hear," the guy said sarcastically.

"This time however we bet against you," Ronald said, stepping up onto the first tier and leaning in real close to the blond and bound Hercules, trailing a finger between the guy's sweat soaked massive cleavage. "That was our good buddy out there that you beat the tar out of in the competition."

"So that's what this is all about?" Hard Pack complained bitterly. "You mugs are sore losers of all things? Fuck man, get these chains off me and be on your way! And maybe, *just maybe* I'll forget this whole escapade of yours."

"It's not all that cut and dry Hard Pack," Ronald said, grabbing the bodybuilder's big pink fleshy nipples in his thumbs and first two

36

fingers, squeezing them hard and as meanly as he had squeezed the guy's crotch just moments ago.

"Arrrrhhhhh fuck, fuck, leave my tits alone you pervert," Hard Pack spat at Ronald.

"Hard Pack my big boy, you are in no position to be telling me or anyone what the fuck we can or can't do with you," Ronald said with a leer and again squeezed the bodybuilder's nipples real hard, getting another good grunt of pain out of him. "You see, like I said, you're about to star in a competition all your own, a twisted and fucked up competition Hard Pack."

Ronald held the guy's nipples real tight in his thumbs and fingers as Alex and I began moving him down off the top tier, forcing him to his feet, pulling on the chains we'd secured around his arms.

"Uuuuuuhhhhhhrrrr, fuckers, sore losers," the guy grunted as we got him off the tier and balanced on his wobbly feet.

He was sweating like mad, every last inch of him glistening with it. Beads of piss had formed on the tip of his wide sexy slit and were dripping on the floor.

"Fuck man, dig this big man cleavage," Ronald said, running the palm of a hand over and over Hard Pack's massive chest, continuing to tweak and squeeze his nipples meanly.

"Come on man, let's get out of here," Alex piped up. "It's hot as hell in this fucking sauna."

"What's the matter faggot, can't take the heat?" Hard Pack said turning and sneering at Alex.

In return Alex gave the guys tight muscular ass cheeks a hard slap which resounded throughout the sauna.

"Owwwwcchhhhh!!!" he seethed. "Fuckers, perverts, get these damned chains off me and then we'll....Ayyyrrrrrr shiiiitttttt..."

But Hard Pack's words were suddenly cut off in mid sentence as Ronald grabbed the guy's manhood as we moved him toward the smoking mineral rocks of the sauna.

"Judging from the way you're dripping and leaking Hard Pack I get the feeling that you really need to relieve yourself," Ronald said, using the guy's dick like a leash as we got him positioned right in front of the steaming rocks.

Hard Pack's body was heaving as Ronald squeezed his manhood real tight, grunting angrily as his dick was held over the hot and steaming rocks.

"Come on muscle guy, come on you big lug, fan these rocks with your piss," Ronald laughed, stroking the guy's now hard and beefy dick.

"Ohhhhrrr fuck man, it, it's goin' to be just a tad more than piss you pranksters," Hard Pack panted and as Ronald stroked the guy he shot a load as big as his muscles. "Ahhhhrrrrr g-gawds, fuckers got me creaming like a bitch in heat in here!!"

We all watched in awe, as the muscle stud seemed to cum and cum as Ronald stroked him and stroked him.

"Fuck man, I didn't mean to make the guy shoot his load," Ronald laughed as Hard Pack's jazz landed and sizzled on the hot rocks.

The smell of his juices cooking filled the hot air and Alex and I stole squeezes of his perfectly proportioned butt cheeks. Ronald stroked and stroked until every last drop of mess that the guy had was spurted from his meat stick. "Hard Pack" was breathless and wordless for the moment, while Ronald forced him to jazz and jazz.

Then, still holding "Hard Pack's" semi hard dick Ronald made the guy piss, as originally intended.

"F-fucking perverts, Ahhhhhhhhh…" Hard Pack breathed heavily as his yellow stream landed on the sauna rocks as well.

"Man oh man, it's smelling like cooked bodybuilder in here," Ronald snickered, giving the guys dick a few strokes as he pissed and pissed.

That got a few good shudders out of "Hard Pack" let me tell you man.

"Getting your sexy ass kidnapped really turns you the fuck on huh Hard Pack?" Ronald asked the trapped bodybuilder and we all laughed meanly. "The way you shot your big creamy wad of spunk really attests to that bud."

"Go on, *laugh, laugh all you want you miserable mugs,*" the bodybuilder seethed more than madly. "But mark my fucking words, when I'm out of these chains you three will pay…*and pay dearly I might add…*"

A few moments later we were lugging the big guy out of the sauna and toward the stairs that would take us back up to the gym. Alex and I were holding the big muscle guy aloft by his upper body while Ronald carried him by his big sweaty feet tucked under his arm.

"Fuckers, *bastards, put me down you guys,*" Hard Pack ranted miserably. "Fucking guys, carryin' me like I was a sack of dirty laundry or something…"

"That's sure how you smell Hard Pack," Alex snickered.

"Yeah, I'll second that," Ronald quipped, hoisting the bodybuilder's bare feet higher under his arm. "These feet of his sure stink to the high heavens."

"Fucking shitty way to be talking about me you mugs," Hard Pack complained.

At the stairs we had no choice but to put the guy down, unless we wanted to attempt to carry over two hundred pounds of hard muscle up them. Alex and I again hauled him along by the chains on his upper arms, this time up the stairs. The muscle stud did his best on the stairs not to be moved upward and to hold his ground that is until Ronald meanly jammed a finger high up into the guy's sweaty and randy asshole.

"Ayyyyyrrrrrrr fucccckkkkk, *faggot!!*" Hard Pack seethed, turning and looking at Ronald with fire and hatred in his eyes. "Gawd man, *get your goddamned finger out of my stinking hole you bastard!!*"

"Move along like my buddies want you to and I won't have to finger and prod your damned raunchy hole bud," Ronald replied and slid a second finger into Hard Pack's mangy hole.

"Ayyyyyrrrrrr shiiiittttt," the guy garbled and this time when we pulled on the chains he moved along, reluctantly, but he moved along.

He breathed a small sigh of relief when Ronald extracted his fingers from his hole…

"Fuck man, I'll eat and fuck that mangy hole of yours like a hungry dog if you don't move your helpless and chained up ass," Ronald threatened and Hard Pack gulped.

Actually, "Hard Pack" didn't have an iota of a clue of just how much his sexy ass would suffer that day, in more ways than one let me tell you.

When we got up to the gym the three of us again hoisted the big guy off his feet and carried him over to the free weights area so we could avoid having to pull and yank on the chains on his arms. It was the same area of the gym where he'd less than an hour or so ago won his latest competition…

"Blasted mugs, what are you guys planning on doing to me here?" he babbled angrily.

"Just do as you're told and you'll be fine," Ronald said giving the guys hefted smelly feet a hearty sniff. "Come on guys, let's get busy…"

A few minutes later we had "Hard Pack" bent over a workout horse at the waist, the chains on his arms used to secure him to the handles on the thing. His legs were spread wide and tied off at the ankles to a hundred pound dumbbell each on the floor, his hole wide open, pink, stinking and gaping. As Ronald stood behind the guy prodding his mangy hole with three fingers this time Alex and I handed the guy two hundred pounds of weights on a bar. He held the bar tightly and in agony in his manacled hands.

"Arrrhhhhh gawd, f-fuckers…" Hard Pack seethed as he took the weight from us.

"Now you just hold onto that, do as you're told and you'll be fine," Alex said as he and I let go of the weight bar.

"Damn it man, fucking guy back there just loves my damned stinking hole!!" Hard Pack garbled, trying to twist his head around and look angrily at Ronald.

"More than you could know Hard Pack,' Ronald said, slid his fingers out of the guy's hole and shucked his shorts down along with his underpants.

Hard Pack gulped loud and faced forward, a look of utter dismay on his handsome face. Ronald's dick was mammoth sized and hard as a rock ready to plow "Hard Pack's" hole like a field.

"No, no, not this you bastard!!" Hard Pack pleaded through quivering lips as Ronald pressed the crown of his hardness against the walls of Hard Pack's waiting hole.

"Start hefting that weight my buddies were good enough to give you, you muscle bound asshole," Ronald said and gave the guys ass cheeks two hard whacks each.

Alex and I stepped to Ronald's sides as Hard Pack did as he had just been told. As he began hoisting the super-heavy weight bar slowly up and down Ronald slid his hardness into the poor guys hole, good and fucking deep and with no lubricant whatsoever.

"Ayyyrrrrrrrr ohhhhrrrr fucccckkkkk!!!" Hard Pack screamed, throwing his head back and looking up at the ceiling.

"Oh yeah, that's the word you gorgeous stud, *fuck,*" Ronald gasped. "Fuck man, your hole is sucking my dick inside you Hard Pack old boy."

With a look of ecstasy on his face Ronald slapped the guys butt cheeks some more, harder and harder and plowed into him deeper and deeper.

"Ohhhhhrrrr you scum bag, you low life, slob!!" Hard Pack ranted and lifted the weight as he was fucked and fucked.

"Damn it you guys, I'm in so fucking deep I'm touching his shit," Ronald laughed, grabbed the guys hips and thrust in and out like a man possessed.

After Ronald shot his load deep inside the bodybuilder's hole it was Alex's turn. Ronald's dick slid out of the now cum soaked hole and Alex wasted no time.

"Ohhh man feels so warm and squishy in here," Alex said in ecstasy and like Ronald pushed himself good and deep inside the trapped bodybuilder.

While Alex fucked the muscle stud he started to falter with the weight and pleaded with us to let him put it down. Instead Ronald and I were good enough to spot him for a few reps while Alex plowed the guy from behind.

"Ohhhhrrrr gawd, y-you guys are going to pay for this," Hard Pack spat at Ronald and I as we stood in front of him assisting in lifting the weight. "And pay dearly, see if I'm kidding!!"

"Shut your yap and keep lifting you muscle freak," Ronald chided the guy. "Or else I'll cram my damned stinking underpants deep in your mouth.

Hard Pack gulped again shut his mouth and we let go of the weight bar. He struggled erotically to lift and lift while Alex plugged him deeper and deeper. The sounds of the chains jangling filled the air around us. It took Alex slightly longer than it did for Ronald to shoot his load, but after he was done it was my turn. Hard Pack looked miserable as I stepped behind him and entered him inch by painful inch...

The three of us fucked the trapped bodybuilder three times each. When I pulled out of him after my second go he uncontrollably let out a loud watery and smelly fart. That got all of us laughing real meanly. His dick was semi hard between his spread legs and again we laughed as he pissed long and yellow on the floor. He called us all sorts of horrible things as he pissed and pissed his hole twitching and sore behind him as he relieved himself on the floor. By the time we were done his hole was dripping with our mess, landing on the floor behind him along with his piss. I'm not ashamed to say that we each ate his hole a few times to sample his stink and each other's juices...

He swore and cursed like a true marine through it all...

A few minutes later we had hauled the guy over to a chin-up bar. His arms weakened by the way we'd made him lift the two hundred pounds while we took our turns fucking him there wasn't all that much he could to do to stop us moving him into the new position we had chosen for him.

"You're lucky I didn't make you lick your mess of piss off the floor Hard Pack old boy," Ronald teased the guy as Alex and I got the chains on his arms secured over and onto the chin-up bar above him.

"Fucking perverts, that's what you three are," Hard Pack grumbled as Ronald took a handful of his again hard dick.

"What's this Hard Pack?" Ronald laughed, grabbing one of the guy's ass cheeks at the same time he started stroking him. "Enjoying all this shit huh?"

"Ohhhhh no, no, not again you blasted mug, oh gawds, I-I'm going to shoot my fucking load like crazy," Hard Pack panted. "Again..."

That said "Hard Pack" let go with another good gusher of bodybuilder juices.

"Ohhhhrrrrr gawd," he panted as Ronald squeezed his ass cheek and stroked him and stroked him.

Hard Pack's juices landed all thick and sloppy on the floor in front of him...

"Looks like you were right Ronald," I said gleefully. "Being kidnapped really does get this guy going."

"Yeah, well never mind that," Ronald said, letting go of Hard Pack's manhood. "Alex, go and get three racquet ball paddles."

Hard Pack looked angrily at Ronald.

"You my big boy are in for a spanking," Ronald said and brazenly gave one of the bodybuilder's nipples a mean slurp.

Then, a few moments later the sounds of the racquet ball paddles connecting hard with "Hard Pack's" bare bottom as he hung from the chin-up bar filled and echoed through the gym.

"OWWWCHHH!!!" the guy gasped and gasped as we took turns swatting his muscular sexy butt cheeks over and over. "OWWWWRRR!!!"

His manacled wrists were pulled over his head exposing his blond tufted sweaty and stinky armpits. While Alex and Ronald swatted and swatted his ass cheeks I paid his armpits some attention. Standing in front of the guy I sniffed and even licked at them. Each time he was swatted from behind his chained up body jerked forward and back in sync with the rhythm of the blows he was receiving.

"How many have we given him so far?" Alex asked Ronald.

"Who's counting?" Ronald laughed and then my two buddies were each swatting one of Hard Pack's ass cheeks over and over at the same time, harder and harder with each blow.

"RRRRRRRRRRR!!!" the bodybuilder seethed through clenched teeth. "Fuck, fuck, slimy perverts, and this fucking guy is licking my damned pit!!"

"Ha, just wait till you see what we have in mind for you next Hard Pack ol' boy," Ronald laughed and gave poor Hard pack's ass cheeks a few hard swats in fast succession.

By the time we were done spanking and swatting his ass cheeks Hard Pack was a sweating and sniveling mess, not to mention that his ass cheeks were crimson. I swear I could see them twitching as

Alex and I got the chains undone from the chin-up bar we had hung him from.

"Okay guys, lets get him stretched out on that bench over there," Ronald said and the three of us again hoisted the guy off the floor.

This time he didn't seem to mind being carried along by us...

We quickly got him lying on his back and stretched out on a long bench. Above him was a weight bar with over two hundred pounds of mass on it, prepared by us especially for our fine catch of the day. Standing over him Alex and I watched as Ronald unhooked the short slack of chain on Hard Pack's wrist manacles from the chains secured around his torso.

"Okay Hard Pack, I want at least ten good reps out of you before we let you off this bench," Ronald said sternly, squatting at the guys side, really drinking in the sight of the trapped bodybuilder.

"Fucking bastards, you guys have kidnapped me, chained me up like some wild animal, fucked my asshole, gawd, *you scum bags fucked my asshole,*" Hard Pack complained and as he spoke Ronald smiled meanly and again began stroking his big dick. "You spanked me red and made me lift a dangerous amount of weights and now... ohhhrrrr fuck, I-I'm goin' to shoot my damned load all over again you bastard!"

Lying on the bench "Hard Pack" reached up, grabbed the weight bar and shot his load again, this time all over his chained up massive body...

"Stop itemizing what we've done to you and start hefting that weight asshole," Ronald said and let go of the guy's dick.

The three of us stood around the bench watching as "Hard Pack" suffered through the chest presses. If he couldn't get through a rep two of us would be there to spot him. We were just having some mean fun with the guy after all. We didn't want him winding up in a hospital.

"Ohhhhhrrrrrr fuccckkkk," Hard Pack screamed like a banshee when he got to the ninth rep. "I can feel that shit in my balls…"

When he completed the tenth and last rep he deposited the weight bar back on the rack behind him and again pissed uncontrollably. It mixed with the mess of sweat and jazz all over his chest, the scent of it wafting up at us erotically.

"Go get a few bottles of mineral water out of the machine by the door," Ronald said to Alex and I. "He needs it now."

Alex and I walked over to the machine to get "Hard Pack" the much-needed water.

"Enjoying yourself?" Ronald teased the guy and took his manacled wrists in his hands.

Before "Hard Pack" could make a move to struggle or even better to club Ronald a hard one Ronald got the short slack of the chain again secured to the chains wrapped around the guy's upper body.

"Fucker," Hard Pack whispered in total frustration.

We made the sweaty and stinking guy scoff down three quart-sized bottles of cold mineral water while he sat on the bench where he'd just bench pressed. As we fed him the water his Adam's apple bobbed up and down and the muscles in his shoulders, chest and arms flexed under the tight chains.

"Man, he's really going to be pissing when this is all over," Alex mused, holding a bottle to the guy's lips.

"Yeah, in there next," Ronald said, pointing.

Alex and I looked to where Ronald was pointing and so did "Hard Pack." The guy gulped around a mouthful of water...

When the bodybuilder was well hydrated the three of us lifted him off the bench and carried him to the massage and herbal wrap room...

No, no, I just cooked myself downstairs you bastards," the guy complained loudly as we got him aboard the table in the room.

Ronald turned up the heat under the large tub of hot towels...

"We can't wrap him in the hot towels with the chains on him guys," Ronald said. "We could scald him that way seeing as the chains will heat up."

"So what are you saying that we have to take the chains off him?" I asked nervously.

"Unless you don't want to herbal wrap him," Ronald said.

"Yeah, go ahead, take the chains off me," Hard Pack insisted, lifting his handsome head up off the table and scowling at all of us meanly. "I swear to God I'll take the three of you all at once!"

Ronald stepped over to the tub of hot towels as the herbal mixture they were in began to simmer.

"I've got an idea," Ronald said.

He stepped back over to Hard Pack, grabbed the guy by a handful of his blond hair and punched him good and hard one time across the face.

"Yuuuhhhhfffff!!!" the guy gasped, totally startled and fell into a stupor of sorts.

"Get the chains off him," Ronald said pulling on a pair of rubber gloves and stepping back over to the tub of heating towels.

"Man, that was a shitty thing to do to him," Alex laughed as he and I worked at the getting the chains and manacles off the bodybuilder.

"Well, it'll be worse for us if you guys don't move faster," Ronald said, pulling a steaming towel from the heated mixture in the tub, the scent of minerals and herb filling the small room. "He's going to come to any second. He's a tough fucker. It'll take more than one punch to keep him down, mark my words."

Alex and I quickly got the big guy stretched out on his back on the table, his arms feeling like iron as we handled him.

"Uhhhhhhh…" Hard Pack moaned and as he slowly came to Ronald stood next to him with the hot steaming towel at the ready.

"Okay, both of you get a towel each out of that tub," Ronald said. "But make sure you've got rubber gloves on.

When Hard Pack opened his eyes and took in the sight of Ronald standing there with the towel he was ready to bolt from the tabletop. But alas, Ronald was just too fast for the poor trapped bodybuilder. As the guy made his move to sit up Ronald dropped the hot towel on him, steaming all the fight instantly out of him.

"Ohhhhhhhhh shiiiitttt, Hard Pack grumbled and lay back on the table as Ronald got the heated towel wrapped over him. "Oh fuck, no, no, no…"

Hard Pack grimaced miserably under the towel as Alex and I placed our towels atop the one already on him.

"Damn, with these towels on him we don't need to keep him chained up," I said, getting my towel tucked under the guy as large and thick beads of sweat formed on his forehead.

"Uhhhhhhhh, no, no, don't cook me you bastards," Hard Pack whimpered under the towels.

Ronald extracted another towel from the tub and laid it over Hard Pack's massive bulk. The guy gasped and panted for breath, looking up at us pleadingly.

"Well Hard Pack, I must say, it's been real," Ronald said, leering down at the guy, his muscular body beautifully and erotically outlined under the thin hot towels. "I guess we'll see you at your next competition."

Ronald took "Hard Pack's" bikini out of his back pocket, wiped off the guy's forehead with it and we all exited the massage room, Alex and I carrying the chains we had snagged the big bodybuilder in.

"Will he be okay by himself in there?" I asked Ronald as we walked out.

"Sure, once the towels cool down he'll be able to be on his way," Ronald said, sniffing the bikini heartily. "He'll be exhausted but he'll be on his way…"

It was a half-hour later when "Hard Pack" emerged naked and sweat sopped from the massage room. Cursing and swearing under his breath he walked slowly down the stairs to the locker room area, his butt cheeks beet red. When he got to the locker room he smiled from ear to ear when he saw me sitting on a bench in front of his locker…

"So, did my buddies and I make your fantasy a reality enough for you Hard Pack?" I asked him.

Still smiling he walked over to me, grabbed me by my arms and hoisted me into his arms.

"Better than reality," he said and kissed me sloppily on the cheek. "Just make sure those two buddies of yours are at my next competition. I want my bikini back…"

We both laughed loudly as "Hard Pack" headed for the showers…

Alex, Working the Late Shift at the Inn

I was out having a grand time on a recent Saturday night when this occurred. It was I, Ron and my other pal Howard. We had just been to see a film at a theater which was in walking distance to my apartment when I suggested we stop at a nearby inn for a beer or two before heading home. I figured being that none of us were driving there was no harm in a pint or two. My two buddies agreed heartily. Fuck, Ron even offered to buy the first round. We walked in the warm September air to the inn not too far from my place called "The Lion's Head." It was a trifle after midnight and the place was not all that crowded. I saw some empty tables scattered about as we entered. The inn was dimly lit, as any proper inn should be. It was done up in the style of a real nineteenth century Irish inn of sorts. Cigar and cigarette smoke filled the air. A long bar adorned the side of the place with a pool table set way in the back, the only modern device in the whole place. Small tables were set up around the front of the place for patrons who preferred not to sit at the bar. We stood at the door waiting for the big bloke sitting at the front podium to come and seat us. At the moment he was busy processing another three guy's check. The podium he was seated at was set up with a cash register on it. The bloke was seated on a barstool. Glancing over at him I saw that he was a bald headed chap with a thick dark goatee. He wore spectacles and from where we were standing I saw that he had very dark and intense looking eyes behind those specs. He was clad in the traditional inn worker's uniform of a white long sleeved shirt, a black necktie and black trousers. His feet propped on the rung of the stool he was seated on were clad in burgundy loafers and ribbed black sheer socks. *Fuck, at the sight of those sheer socks my heart did a double whammy in my chest.* The bloke finished with the guys paying their bill and glanced over at us.

"Table for three gentlemen?" he asked us in a baritone sounding tone of voice.

"Yes Sir," Ron replied as the bloke got up off his barstool.

He stepped over to us and as he did I guessed his height to be close to six feet tall. His upper body really filled up his white shirt with nicely toned muscles, from what I could see.

"Right over here guys," he said, indicating a small square table, which was very near to his podium.

"Thanks bud," Howard said.

For whatever the reason I made sure to take the seat that was facing the podium where I knew the bloke would be re-seated any second, seeing as there were two women standing there waiting to pay their bill now.

"Enjoy your evening guys," the bloke said with a smile, looking directly at me for a few seconds. "My name is Alex. I'm the headwaiter, along with being the cashier and the dishwasher and the bottle boy and..."

We all chuckled at his little joke.

"Basically, if you need anything don't hesitate to call me," Alex said with a grin.

"Looks like you have to be a jack of all trades in this place eh mate?" Ron asked Alex, giving the head waiter's black tie a playful tug.

"Sure as shit gents," Alex said and in response straightened his tie in a workaholic fashion. "Enjoy yourselves. A waiter will be with you momentarily."

He stepped back over to his podium, sat up on his barstool and again propped his big feet on the lowest rung of the stool. Again, I couldn't help noticing the black ribbed sheer socks the guy was wearing. The way his trousers rode up when he sat down gave me more than a good view of the pretty socks. Looking at them on him my heart again thundered madly in my chest. What was up with that anyway? But then, my thoughts were cut short as a waiter came over to our table.

"Good evening gents," the blond guy said smiling, his check pad and pen ready. "What can I get for you tonight?"

I nearly said "The headwaiter's socks," but quickly bit my tongue.

"Three pints of Bass ale on draft please," Ron replied.

"Coming right up," the waiter said, jotted down the order and walked to the bar.

Once again my eyes were riveted to Alex's feet on the rungs of his barstool. He was again taking care of another group's check.

"This place does some business eh mate?" Howard asked me, looking at me across the table and turning to steal a glance at the headwaiter. "Seems like that bloke is never not busy."

"Yeah, it sure would seem that way," I replied, still looking at Alex's socks as he worked the cash register.

He wished the patrons he'd just rung up a good night and then glanced over at me. I wasn't quick enough to avert my eyes from where they were staring and I was sure the bloke caught me checking out his socks. He smiled pleasantly at me and turned his attention back to his post.

"So, what did you guys think of the movie?" I asked, trying to make some normal conversation while at the same time wanting to figure out my fascination with the headwaiter's damned socks.

"I thought it was okay, a little slow to get to the point, but otherwise I enjoyed it," Ron said, leaning back in his chair, not realizing that by doing so he was giving me a better view of Alex's feet.

"I agree mate," Howard piped up. "The story in the movie could have been told in less time. That way we could have been here sooner and already drinking beer."

We all laughed at Howard's remark. Yeah, we could have been here sooner and looking at the headwaiter's socks I thought. But God, I wanted more than just to look at them man... For the briefest of moments I thought how those sheer socks would smell by night's end. That thought, was followed by imagining those socks in a plastic zip lock bag, to be kept by me forever...

Just then the blond waiter appeared carrying a round tray with three pints of Bass ale on it.

"Here we are guys," he said, placing a glass each in front of us.

"Thanks bud," Ron said and handed the guy a twenty. "I don't need the change."

"Thanks Sir, I'll be along soon when you're ready for the next round," the waiter said and walked off.

"To friendship," Ron said and held up his glass.

"To friendship," Howard and I repeated and we all clinked our glasses together.

I glanced over at Alex. He smiled at me, raised a glass of water that he'd been sipping and helped himself. I smiled back at him, although my two buddies thought I was smiling with them. We discussed the movie we had seen further and then talked about other general things like work, the economy and what was happening in the world of sports. As we talked and sipped our beers I continued stealing glances over at Alex's feet. Those black ribbed sheer socks of his had a hold on me that I could not believe. Again he happened to look over at me and caught me at it, looking at his feet, that is. When I was too late to turn away he reached down to scratch an itch he supposedly had on his upper calf. He hiked his pants leg up, revealing the top of his sheer sock, showing some leg skin as he scratched. I got the distinct feeling that he wanted me to know that his socks were calf-length. Finished with his itch he let his pants leg fall back down and he turned his attention back to the customers who'd just come up to pay their bill.

"Looks like you're always busy mate," I heard one of the young men say to Alex as he processed their check.

"Yeah, they work me hard here," Alex replied with a grin. "They sure as shit make me sweat in my socks, that is for sure."

I nearly blanched as he said that loud enough for me to hear. While we were on our second round of beers I began thinking about this whole thing with the headwaiter's socks. I am totally heterosexual, always been attracted to females, all sorts of females to be perfectly frank. But God man, there was something about this guy and his sheer socks that was driving me batty. I admit I had a boner in my trousers the size of a fucking python. As we sipped our beers and chatted Alex suddenly made his way over to us.

"Enjoying yourselves, guys?" he asked us, standing behind my two buddies and looking intently at me, his dark eyes intense behind his specs.

"Oh yeah, everything is fine," Ron replied. "Good service, good beer…"

"Good, I'm glad to hear it," Alex said. "I'm glad the place is starting to quiet down now though. I don't think I've stopped working once since I got here at seven o'clock."

"Yeah mate, like I heard you say, they really make you sweat in your socks here," Howard said.

"That they do," Alex said, glancing at me and grinning.

"You uh, work here full time?" I asked him.

"No, this is just something I do when I need some extra money," Alex replied. "I work as a detective full time."

"Whoa, now that sounds exciting!" Howard chirped and we all raised our glasses. "To Alex the detective."

"I'll bet being a detective makes you sweat like crazy in your socks," I boldly said.

"Hmmm, not as much as they make me sweat here," Alex responded. "Well, I better check on what's left of the patrons here and get back to my post."

He again walked off…

By the time we were finished with our third rounds of beer it was after three AM and we were the last three people in the inn, along with Alex the head waiter that is.

"Man, we better be on our way," Howard said. "I didn't realize it was so late."

"Me either," Ron said, reaching for the check that the blond waiter had left on the table. "Lets tally up our check here and get going."

"I'll take care of it," I said, swiping the check up off the table. "You already paid for the first round Ron. I'll take care of what's left."

"Are you sure mate?" Ron asked, getting to his feet.

"Sure, you guys go on, I live real close by," I said. "I'll call you tomorrow."

"Okay then, have a good sleep mate," Howard said and we all shook hands.

When Ron and Howard were gone I picked up the check and walked slowly over to Alex. He was sitting on his barstool, one of his feet halfway out of his shoe. I noticed that the heel part of his sock was not sheer, but totally black. I would soon learn what TNT socks were...

"Last one for the night I suppose," I said, still stealing glances at those sheer socks of his, the boner in my trousers not quitting.

"That you are," Alex said, sliding his foot into his loafer.

I stepped next to his podium rather than in front of it, wanting as much of a sight as possible of the handsome bloke's pretty socks. With my hand trembling I handed him the check for the beers that the waiter hadn't taken money for.

"So, did you and you buddies have a nice time here?" Alex asked me, taking the check from me and pecking at the cash register keys.

"Yeah, we sure did," I replied and looked down at his feet.

"Did you drop something?" Alex asked me, looking down as well.

"I, I thought I did," I said, needing an excuse for what I was about to do.

Actually, I could not believe what the fuck I was about to do.

"Well, take a closer look," Alex said, placing my tallied check on tip of the cash register. "Maybe whatever you dropped slid under my podium here."

"Yeah, sure," I said softly and squatted down slowly, till I was looking directly at Alex's feet on the lowest rung of his stool.

"Is it down there?" he asked, knowing that I hadn't dropped anything, knowing that I wanted more than just a glance at his socks this time.

"I, uh, I don't think so, perhaps I was wrong," I said, not looking up at him, but instead looking at his feet, just inches away from me now.

"I don't think you were wrong," Alex said, looking down at me.

"Say bud, wh-where'd you get these real fancy socks you got on?" I asked him, boldly hooking a hand around the ankle part of his foot nearest to me.

"You like them?" Alex asked me, and I could feel him grinning down at me.

"Honestly, yeah mate, I think they're really nice," I replied, him not protesting as I pulled his foot off the rung and toward me.

I could not fucking believe it, I now had the big blokes foot in my hand. His foot felt strong and meaty in my hand, a real man's foot let me tell you.

"I like the sheerness of them, for whatever the reason," I said, trailing a finger of my other hand between two of the ribs. "Man, I can even see the hair on your legs through them."

I moved my hands together around his calf, loving the feel of his sheer socks against his strong sexy leg.

"There's a store downtown in the shopping area," Alex said. "It's a shoe store, but as luck would have it they have a good selection of men's socks as well. I like these the best because they're TNTs."

"TNTs mate?" I asked, pulling his foot still closer to me, running a hand under his pants leg, finding the top of his sock at his calf and snapping it against his skin.

"Nice tight elastic," I said. "Helps 'em to stay up while you sweat in them I suppose."

"Yeah, that's true," Alex said with a grin. "Anyway, TNT means thick and thin."

"Thick and thin?" I asked, still not understanding.

With his foot still in my hands Alex turned and faced forward on the stool, the fronts of his feet now facing me.

"Thick and thin means that the toes, heels and topmost parts of the socks are solid black silk, not sheer like the part you're seeing right now," Alex explained. "Take one of my loafers off and you'll see what I mean."

Take one of his loafers off? *Take one of his loafers off?* Man, I couldn't believe that the guy was letting me hold his foot in my hand, now he wanted me to take one his loafers off? I fleetingly wondered where this exchange was leading.

"O-okay Mate," I said and still holding his foot with one hand (God, I didn't ever want to let go of it) I took his loafer off slowly by the heel with my other hand.

As I took his loafer off at the heel first I saw what he meant, what I'd seen just moments ago while he'd had his foot slipped out of his loafer, that the heel section of his sock was solid black silk. With my breath coming slowly I slid his loafer the rest of the way off, revealing that the toe section of his sock was solid black silk also.

"Oh, now I see what you mean," I said, staring in awe at his sheer socked foot, the musty odor of it wafting upward and filling my nostrils.

I inhaled deeply and the boner in my trousers pounded harder.

"Get my other shoe off as well, you'll really get the full effect and see how nice those socks look on my big smelly feet," he suggested.

"Ah, they don't smell that bad mate," I said, looking up at him with a grin on my face.

"Don' think so bud?" he asked me. "Remember what I said before, the way they work me here really makes me sweat in my socks. Sniff the inside of that loafer you're still holding if you don't believe me."

Fuck man; sniff the inside of the guy's shoes? But I couldn't resist. I just had to do it. I placed the inside of his loafer over my nose and mouth and inhaled deeply, the scent of foot sweat, sock silk and leather filling my nose. My eyes rolled in my head…in ecstasy.

"See what I mean bud?" he asked me. "Stinks huh?"

I nodded.

"Yeah, fucking guys who run this place really make me sweat in my damned socks," he said, sounding frustrated. "Go ahead bud, put that shoe down and get the other one off me as well. You'll see that the inside of that one is just as smelly."

I could have said that I would take his word for it, but instead I did as he said. Still holding his foot in hand by the ankle I placed his loafer on the floor and got busy getting his other one off. He watched intently, staring down at me as I slowly slid his other shoe off at the heel. When it was off he wriggled his toes in his socks and without being told to do so I quickly inhaled the odor of the inside of his second shoe.

"Real musty and funky," I said with the shoe over my nose and mouth.

I quickly put the shoe down alongside the first one and hooked my hands around one of his feet each at the ankles as they rested on the rung of the barstool, pointing straight at me.

"But it's these socks of yours that really got my attention mate," I said, moving my face closer to his feet without realizing I was doing so.

I moved my hands over the tops of his feet and snared the toe's sections of his both his socked feet in my fingers and thumbs.

"Say man, do you mind if I..." I said, almost panting, my heart racing. "I mean, would you think me weird if I..."

As I spoke, pleaded and nearly begged I was looking intently at the guy's socked feet. My tongue was practically hanging out. My face was less than mere inches from his wiggling socked toes.

"Go ahead bud," he said to me and I could feel him smiling knowingly down at me. "Seems like most guys, even straight as they are sometimes want to do to my socked feet what you're about to do."

Without another word I pulled one of his feet off the rung of his stool and wrapped my lips eagerly around his moist socked toes. The taste was musty and funky to say the least, but I had the guy's socked toes in my mouth. That thought alone sent me into a frenzy of sorts. He wiggled his toes in my mouth as I moved my hands up his socked calves, loving, adoring the feel of his sheer socks against his muscular strong leg. I sucked heartily at the moistness of his toes, wishing I could get more of his foot in my mouth. Each time I swallowed I was treated to a mouth and throat full of Alex's delicious foot stink.

"Mmmm…that feels real nice bud," Alex said softly and I glanced up at him.

He was looking down at me with a grin of ecstasy on his handsome face.

"Oh man, oh mate," I said, letting his toes slip out of my mouth for a second, but not once letting go of his foot as I spoke. "Like you said, I'm straight as a fucking arrow, but there is something about these feet of yours in your sheer socks."

"I know what you mean bud," he said almost lovingly and then gently urged his socked toes back into my mouth. "One time a guy took such a shine to my socked feet that he kept me tied to his bed for hours in a spread eagle in just my socks. Fucking guy sucked and slurped my feet for hours while he had me there."

"Oh yeah mate," I whispered and quickly clamped my lips around his socked toes again.

The thought of this big handsome bloke all roped to my bed while I worked his socked feet was enough to get me sucking harder still on his toes…

When I had sucked and slurped all I could of his scent out of his first foot I slid the socked toes of his other foot into my mouth and went to work on that one next. Glancing up at the guy as he sat there relaxed on his stool I saw the boner he was sporting in his trousers.

"Mmmm…" he crooned. "Feels so good the way you're sucking and licking my toes…"

I swirled my tongue over and over the arches of his feet, holding them tight by the heels at this point. I even found myself gently kissing the tops of his big feet. The veins in his feet showed through the sheerness of his socks and I glided my tongue along those, sending obvious chills and thrills through the guy… He shuddered on his stool…

"Looks like it's me who has you sweating in your socks now, eh mate?" I asked him, flicking my tongue up his socked calf, pushing his trouser leg up as I did so, the scent emanating from his feet unbelievable at that point.

"Would sure seem like it bud," he agreed.

"Can't get enough," I said breathlessly.

"Me either bud, me either," he panted just as breathlessly.

"Then I guess we'll just have to do something about that now won't we?" I asked, reluctantly letting go of his feet and standing up

"What do you have in mind bud?" he asked me as I tugged at the knot in his tie, looking intently into his dark eyes.

"Well, lets take care of my bill and head over to my apartment," I said with as much authority as I could muster. "As I said I don't live all that far from here."

"What I told you gave you ideas huh bud?" he asked me.

"Sure as shit mate," I replied, not letting go of his tie. "And I have plenty of rope I could use on you..."

He seemed to consider what I just said and turned to his cash register.

"Your bill is on me," he said, pecking away at the keys. "Fuck man, so many of you foot fetishists want to tie me the fuck up..."

As he spoke, pecking away at the keys he was grinning widely from ear to ear...

I glanced down at his socked feet resting on the rung of his stool...

I slowly slid back to my knees and this time started from behind him, licking and lapping at his heels...

It was hours before I got the handsome bloke to my apartment...

On the Beach

What I should have done was titled this "How I spent a summer day back in 1996. I can't believe it took this long to finally decide to write it all down. But with all the guys out there talking and bragging about the erotic experiences they've had I guess I just felt that I should finally let my voice be heard. Let me tell you about it. My name is Rivers, Brad Rivers to be exact. I'm a dark haired, well-muscled, smooth chested six-foot tall guy. I work as an account representative and customer service manager for a bank in Manhattan. On a Wednesday in the heated month of August I decided to shuck the (monkey) business suit, the tie, the wing tip shoes and the knee length black nylon socks and to take the day off. I hadn't had a day off in over eight months and figured I truly deserved it. I decided to spend the day alone on the beach. I packed a lounge chair into my car along with suntan oil and a pair of dark glasses. Dressed in shorts, a tee shirt, canvas slip-on shoes and a black Speedo bikini under my shorts I drove to the beach in Brooklyn. It was mid morning so I found a parking spot pretty easily one block from the beach. I walked down to the beach with my lounge chair under my arm and my suntan oil in my hand. When I found the perfect spot on the sand I set up my lounge chair kicked off my canvas shoes, stripped to my Speedo bikini and quickly sat down being that the sand was extremely hot. As I slathered suntan oil over my muscular body I looked around. Being that it was a weekday the beach was pretty much deserted. In the distance I was able to see an elderly couple sitting on beach chairs. Lucky them I thought, they probably get to come here everyday in the summer. Poor mugs like me are trapped behind desks clad in a business suit and being choked by what has come to be called a power tie. Enjoying my privacy and my day off I sat back on my lounge chair, closed my eyes and soaked up the sun's rays. An hour or so went by and I dozed on and off, but then I heard voices approaching. I opened my eyes and saw three big guys coming down onto the beach. I was groggy from the heat and sweating like crazy. My body glistened from the combination of sweat and suntan oil.

"So much for privacy," I thought, taking off my dark glasses.

I watched as the three guys set up their chairs, a large beach umbrella and some towels on the hot sand not too far from where I was sitting stretched out on my lounge chair. They were all very tall and very muscular. I could tell that they, like me, spent a lot of time at the gym lifting weights. They all had brown hair cut really short. I wondered also if they, like me were playing hooky from their jobs. One of them noticed me and waved over, being real friendly like, greeting me. I waved back. After they were done setting up their gear they came over to me, all stripped to their bathing suits and canvas shoes.

"Good morning," one of them said to me.

"Good morning to you," I replied, looking up at them. "Can I help you guys?"

"We don't seem to have any suntan lotion or oil," the second guy said. "Could we borrow some of yours?"

"No problem," I said and reached under my chair.

I handed the first guy the bottle of suntan oil and he began slathering it all over his muscular and well-toned body.

"Thank you," he said. "My name is Dave. These guys are my good buddies Tony and Frank."

"I'm Brad," I said and held out my hand.

They all reached down to shake hands with me. Then, Tony took the suntan oil and began applying it to his body.

"I think I'll take a dip in the water before I put on that oil," Frank said, looking down at me, almost hungrily I thought. "Care to join me Brad? You look like you could use it. The way you're glistening I'm guessing you've been in the sun more than a while."

"Yeah, I'm pretty much cooked," I said, standing up on my bare feet as Frank slipped his canvas shoes off himself.

"Shit!! The sand is hot!" Frank exclaimed loudly.

"It sure is," I agreed. "We'd better run for the water."

"Gentlemen, let's make this run you're about to do a little interesting," Dave piped up as Frank and I tottered from foot to foot on the hot sand.

"What do you have in mind?" I asked him.

"Knowing this guy it's something totally weird," Frank said to me, giving my shoulder a squeeze.

"What I have in mind is a race to the water between the two of you," Dave said, looking at Frank and I. "The loser has to carry the winner back here atop his shoulders slowly, in the hot sand. From the look of things we all work out pretty hard at the gym so it should be a piece of cake for the loser to do."

"See, I told you," Frank said, his hand still on my shoulder. "Not only weird, but sadistic at the same time."

Frank and I looked at each other, contemplating what Dave had just suggested.

"Do you think you're up for it Brad?" Frank asked me. "I run pretty fast and I'm real muscle heavy."

"You're on," I replied with a friendly looking smirk on my face and Frank took his hand off my shoulder.

Frank and I dashed off toward the water, running at the highest speed possible. Shit, but that sand was fucking hot. I beat him easily to the cool wet sand and gratefully stopped with my feet in the water.

"Ahhhhh," I said, feeling relieved.

Frank came up behind me.

"Looks like you win Brad," he said and without any warning whatsoever he scooped me up off the sand and into his big muscular burly arms. "At least you're not all that heavy."

"Ha, fuck man, I'm as muscle heavy as you are bud," I said jokingly as the guy lugged me toward the water.

He carried me into the water and dropped me into it. It was cold yet very refreshing. I didn't need three guesses to know what Dave, Tony and Frank were up to. I decided to play along with them and have *some real fun* on my day off. Fuck, *I really wanted to enjoy my day off.* And if being carried on some muscle hunk's shoulders in the hot sand was part of the fun so be it I thought happily. I had a feeling that I knew where all this shoulder squeezing, guy carrying and sadistic fun was heading anyway. Frank and I thrashed around playfully in the water. A few times he lifted me into his arms and threw me under, dunking me as we called it when I was a kid. I admit I really liked the way his hands felt as they gripped me by my rear end. I could feel his fingers digging into my buns as he again and again hoisted me out of the water.

"Having fun?" I asked him, as he held me aloft in his arms like a groom lifting his bride over the threshold.

"Tons of it," Frank replied, looking dreamily into my eyes and tossed me into the water again.

My dick was hard as a rock and throbbing in my Speedo bikini. I saw Dave and Tony watching us from where they were standing back on the beach. I waved at them, a big smile on my face. As I waved Frank grabbed my arm, bent me over and hoisted me clear across his shoulders, his hand lying on my ass.

Gotcha Brad ol' boy," he said and threw me hard into the water.

After a while more we decided to head back up to the beach. We swam to where we were able to walk and I asked Frank if he was ready. He said he was and squatted down. I climbed up onto his shoulders and he got me balanced.

"Okay bud, across the hot sand and to where your two buddies are waiting," I said, feeling like a hero baseball player up there on his shoulders.

But instead Frank turned around and grinning, walked back into the water.

"H-hey, what are you doing?" I asked him, feigning annoyance. "Fuck, you're going to dunk me again aren't you man?"

When we were where the water was deep enough Frank tossed me off his shoulders. I playfully thrashed around in the water as he grabbed me and again hoisted me up to his shoulders.

"Okay Brad, let's get this show on the road," Frank said.

With his hands wrapped around my ankles Frank walked out of the water and across the hot sand, carrying me. He bitched about how hot the sand was as he carted me along. When we got to my lounge chair Frank put me down and quickly slipped his canvas shoes back on. I sat down on my lounge chair and stretched myself out nice and comfortable, not knowing that I would very soon be hoisted and carted off again.

"The water was great," he said to Dave and Tony. "Nice and invigorating."

"I'll second that," I said from my chair.

I noticed that the elderly couple was gone. Unbelievably the four of us pretty much had the area of the beach we were at to ourselves. I knew that *anything was possible now.* Sure enough, Dave and Tony squatted down at the sides of my lounge chair.

"Say Brad, how about all of us take a swim now?" Dave asked me, stealing a squeeze on one of my big nipples.

"But I just had a swim and you guys were going to cook in the sun," I said. "You both slathered my suntan oil all over yourselves."

"We'll cook in the water," Tony said from the other side of me, giving my other nipple a good squeeze.

"Looks like the cold water caused your man tits to rise Brad," Tony said to me, jiggling and squeezing my hard nipple.

I looked down and sure enough, my nipples were more than erect. I smiled at the two men from side to side and stood up...

"Come on buddy," Frank said. "I'll give you a ride back to the water."

Frank got me up on his shoulders and carried me back toward the water, followed by his two buddies...

As I said, *anything was possible now...*

"Fucking guys man, you three seem to have a fetish for seeing a guy lugged on another guy's shoulders," I said with a grin as we made our way back to the cool water.

In the water the three of us swam out toward a conglomeration of high rocks. We swam behind the large and concealing rocks, no one to see us now. Without a word I got myself seated on a low and large rock, my legs stretched out along the sides of it. Also without a word Dave and Tony propped themselves on the sides of the rock and they each took one of my salt water flavored nipples into their mouth and began working them. They sucked, nipped, chewed and planted tiny delicate kisses on my fleshy man tits. I leaned back on the rock in total ecstasy.

"Ohhhh yeah, yeah, fucking A, work my tits you guys," I said breathlessly. "Feels more than great..."

Frank proceeded to sidle up in front of me on the rock. He pulled my bikini down in the front and my big meat popped out, long, hard, beefy and fat. Pre cum was oozing out of my wide and sexy piss hole. Frank closed his mouth around my erection and started sucking it for all he was worth.

"Ohhhhhhh..." I moaned in heated passion.

I gripped the sides of the rock I was seated on, leaned my head back and closed my eyes as the three men serviced my tits and dick and the sun caressed me with it's rays. Man, was I glad I had taken the day off and decided to go to the beach. Frank suckled my beefy dick like crazy as Dave and Tony gave my man tits a hard workout with their mouths. They closed their front teeth on them and tortured them erotically. Twice, as I was about to shoot my load Frank expertly held me back by taking my throbbing manhood out of his mouth at just the right moment.

"Oh God, you're fucking driving me crazy," I exclaimed breathlessly.

"Just having some fun with you," Frank explained and slurped me quickly back into his mouth.

He resumed sucking the fuck out of my meat stick, even going down on my big bulging balls still in my bikini.

"Oh God, not much longer now, *oh yeah,*" I groaned loudly.

I bucked on the rock as I felt myself getting close and ready to explode. There would be no stopping me this time that was for sure.

"Oh God yeah!!!" I screamed loudly and shot my load.

Frank swallowed as much of my executive jazz as possible, the rest of it landing on my bikini and dribbling out of the sides of his mouth as he went on and on sucking me. Dave and Tony kept on slurping and sucking on my man tits, as I seemed to cum and cum. When I was done shooting my load Frank let my dick slip out of his mouth and Dave and Tony stopped working my nipples. I looked at all three of them, my eyes darting from one of them to the other.

"Fucking amazing," I said breathlessly. "What a great way to spend a day off."

Frank slipped my bikini off me as Dave and Tony got me down off the rock and into the water. As I bobbed around I watched as the three men shed their bathing suits and left them on the big rock along with my bikini. Naked in the water the three men took turns fucking me as we bobbed around out there behind the rocks, totally unseen. Frank held me from behind, his hands wrapped around my waist and his enormous erection deep inside me as Dave and Tony slurped my nipples back into their mouths for another go round.

Frank held me tighter and tighter against himself as he plowed the fuck out of my hole under the water. Dave and Frank held me by my arms as we bobbed in the water as Tony slid his manhood into me next, after Frank had shot his load deep inside me. Dave stretched himself out on the big rock and Frank and Tony hoisted me up and down on his giant meat stick, making me ride him like a pony as he reamed the fuck out of me. When all three us were spent we sat on the rocks catching our breath. We were sweating like crazy in the hot sun. We all got our bathing suits back on and dived into the water. With our dicks tingling in our bathing suits we swam back to the beach. When we got to the sand Frank got me hoisted onto his shoulders and carried me slowly over the hot sand as Dave and Tony ran off ahead of us.

"Looks like they can't take the hot sand on their feet," I laughed.

"Yeah, if they were carting a load as precious as the one I got on my shoulders they wouldn't mind it so much," Frank said and my heart thundered in my chest at his words.

Later, I was lying on a blanket with Frank lying next to me. He was absently playing with one of my nipples. Dave and Tony were thrashing around back in the water, enjoying themselves.

"Are they lovers?" I asked Frank.

"Sometimes," he replied and sat up, smiling down at me.

"And you?" I asked him. "Are you sometimes their lover? *Do you have a lover?*"

"I haven't met the right person yet," he said and ran a finger over my lips. "Or maybe now I have…"

We stood up and Frank carried me back to the water.

We've been together ever since.

The Construction Worker's Control Knobs

"Ha, man I'm telling you, a guy's big tits are the control knobs for his dick," I said to my buddy Ronald as we twisted, squeezed and twirled the (tied up) construction worker's fleshy nipples. "Just look at how hard he is now. Fucking muscle dude is dyin' to shoot his load."

"RRRRMMMFFFF!!!" the construction worker growled more than angrily.

"Aren't you big boy? Just dyin' to shoot your load?" I asked the brawny and handsome construction worker, leering lecherously at him as he looked at me with eyes filled with outright rage. "Even though it's two guys giving you the once and twice three times over."

For a brief second I let go of his nipple, only to give his big male cleavage a hard stinging slap and quickly grasped his nipple again.

"GRRRRMMMFFFF!!!" the big studly macho man snarled behind his gag. "RRRRMMMFFFFF!!!"

Actually the gag crammed in his mouth was a stinky and sweat soaked red bandanna that until he had wound up in the position he was now in the construction dude had had in the back pocket of his worn jeans. No doubt he had used that bandanna to mop the sweat off himself more than several times during the hot day at the jobsite that Ronald and I had found (and snagged) him at. To add to muscle boy's misery Ronald and I had each pissed onto the bandanna before we crammed it into his mouth. To keep the bandanna safely tucked in his craw we had tied a good length of rope over it, jamming it in place. Every time the Herculean guy swallowed his spit he was treated to a mouth and throat full of his own rancid body stink and the taste of our sour piss; lousy thing to do to a guy you bet your ass bud.

"Fuck it all Alex, this big lug has better tits than that bitch I'm dating, what the fuck was her name again?" my buddy Ronald asked me meanly, his thumb and first three fingers gripping the young construction dude's nipple real tight.

The big lug's nipples had been worked up to the size of two ripe cherries on his massively muscular chest, courtesy of Ronald and I. Fuck, we had been at it now for a better than an hour, not letting up once on the poor muscle boy's nips. They were swollen and totally fucking erect, hard and as pink as two big pencil erasers on his somewhat hairy chest.

"I can't remember her name at the moment either Ronald my man," I replied, working our prize construction worker's other nipple just as harshly as Ronald was doing with the one he had in his thumb and fingers. "All I can think about right now is this big lug's succulent tits."

"MMMMFFFFF!!!" the muscular dude bellowed.

"Say Big boy, you got a girlfriend of your own somewhere?" I asked the construction worker, teasing and squeezing the very bejesus out of his nipple now, really giving it the business, priming it. "A young, handsome muscular dude like you just has to have a pretty girlfriend."

In response the trapped muscle boy angrily nodded, yes, he had a girlfriend. I squeezed and twisted his nipple harder.

"Ha, I truly wonder what she would say if she saw you now," Ronald laughed meanly.

That said we released the giant's nipples, leaned down and slurped them heartily into our mouths.

"RRRRRRMMMMFFFF!!!" the Adonis like brute growled against his foul tasting gag. *F-fraggots!!"*

Good God almighty, snagging the guy at the jobsite he'd been working at had been easy, *almost too easy actually.* He arched his head back and leaned the top of it against the concrete post we had him tied securely to, his sweat soaked short black hair matted to his head, his Adam's apple jutting out real sexy like. He growled angrily as we slurped his nipples like two hungry nursing babies, nipping at them and teasing them with the tips of our tongues. He seethed madly as we lightly clamped our front-most teeth around his nubs and bit down, slathering them with our tongue tips quickly afterwards and then biting them again. He growled even louder when I closed a hand around his hard and sweaty cock, as it hung out of his piss and sweat stained white under shorts. Blessed as he was in the area of his long and fat beefy cock the muscle boy wasn't thrilled about having some joke playing guy handling him down there, although his pre cum dripping hard-on said otherwise. His juicy balls, slightly hairy, sweaty, packed tight and piss scented hung low under his hardness, pressed against his under shorts as he stood there helplessly being used as a sex toy. His worn jeans were pushed down to his knees and his feet were in a big box we had found at the site, the box blocking his view from the surprise that was to come when we were done with him. The muscle boy was roped to the concrete post at the construction jobsite with his big muscular arms pulled around it and roped tight at the wrists behind him. His upper body was securely roped to the post, the ropes pulled tight and wound under his big male cleavage, keeping his massively muscular chest jutting straight up and out for our pleasures. He squirmed erotically and all sweaty in the tight bondage. His booted feet were immobilized and immured in a cardboard box, as I said preventing him from seeing the surprise he was in for when we were finished with him. The four covers of the box were closed and folded over around his muscular calves. The kid was in his early twenties, a real young well-muscled construction dude.

"GGGRRRRRRMMMFFFFF" he reeled even louder when I let go of his sweaty and throbbing cock.

"Oh man, you hated that huh Muscle boy?" I asked him, taking his nipple from my mouth and grabbing it again in my fingers and thumb. "You wanted me to jack you off didn't you, you great big side of beef."

Laughing mockingly I slapped his cleavage real hard, the sound of the sting echoing in the deserted jobsite as I teased his nipple with my fingers and Ronald slurped and sucked his other one.

"Yeah, fuckin' big titted muscle boy wanted me to jack him off didn't you?" I asked him again, grabbing a handful of his man breast and jiggling it real hard. "Fuckin' dude, you hated havin' some guy holdin' your big salami, but now that I've let go of it the feeling is even more intense eh?"

Miserably he nodded "yes" as Ronald and I went for another round of working his nipples with our fingers and thumbs. We squeezed, twisted and twirled the construction dude's beefy man tits; his cock standing straight up and hard as a flag pole...

As we overworked the kid's erect sappy nipples, driving him crazier and crazier I quickly thought about how easy it had all been to snag him...

It was a hot and humid early August evening and Ronald and I were out walking down in the Greenwich Village section in New York City. Ronald, a big brawny thirty something year old guy with brown wavy hair is my best buddy in the whole world. Ever since we were kids we have *always* wreaked havoc on poor unsuspecting dudes like the one I'm telling you about here. It's part of what makes Ronald and I such good buddies, the fact that we're both mean jokers, and the fact that we own one of the sleaziest and busiest bars in New York City. It was just about eight fifteen and the sun was setting. We had a couple of hours before opening our late night bar and we had decided to kill time by walking around the village. As we walked past a large building that was in the throes of construction and renovation on Fourteenth Street Ronald commented that this was going to be the site for that new mini mall that he'd told me about a few weeks ago.

"Wow, it sure is going to be big for a mini mall," I said as we both stopped walking to look at the site.

"Well, actually it was three buildings that are being gutted and made into one big one," Ronald said. "During this past week I passed by here and saw that they were knocking down the walls in there."

"Yeah, and from the sign that I see posted up there it looks like Green and Sons scored another big commission with this project," I said, looking up at the sign on the building.

"Shit man, that construction company seems to be taking over the city," Ronald said. "And from what some of my buddies tell me the guys who work for them make good fucking bucks."

"I suppose if you're going to work in construction then they're the company to work for huh?" I asked.

"Sure as shit buddy, sure as fucking shit," Ronald replied. "I'll tell you, if I worked for a construction company, they're the ones I would want to be employed by. Say, do you want to go in and see how far they've gotten on it?"

"Are you sure we can man?" I replied in question.

"Sure thing, I mean, check it out, the door to the place ain't even locked," Ronald said, pointing to the wooden door standing slightly ajar.

"Maybe the construction crew is still here bud," I said, walking slowly alongside Ronald toward the door.

"I doubt the crew is here at this time Alex," Ronald responded. "Probably they left and just forgot to lock up behind themselves."

We walked into the gutted sidewalk level of the building. It was damp and musty smelling in there, dimly lit by large powered bulbs hanging from different spots in the gutted ceiling. Under our feet dust and chips of cement crunched as we walked.

"Wow, like I said, this is going to be pretty big for a mini mall," I said and at that moment Ronald stopped me in my tracks by suddenly putting his arm up, blocking my path.

"Now we know why the door to this place wasn't closed and locked," Ronald said, pointing at the sound asleep young handsome construction dude.

The kid was sitting on the ground propped against the concrete post we would very soon have him tied tight to. His white sweaty stained tee shirt was off him, lying on the ground beside him, along with three empty beer cans. His head lolled back against the post, making that Adams apple of his jut out real nice and sexy looking. His mouth was wide open and drops of saliva dangled off his lower lip.

"Looks like Sleeping Beauty here decided to have a few cold beers before closing the place up for the night," I said as Ronald and I squatted at the kid's sides as he snored softly.

"Yeah, I bet it was his job to lock the site up and figuring he was the last one here he would sneak a few beers," Ronald said with a mean looking grin on his face.

He truly was a sight to behold let me tell you. He had dark hair, cut very short his bare chest was slightly hairy and extremely muscular. Besides his job as a construction worker I guessed that the kid worked out regularly in a gym, his big muscled arms and broad shoulders attested to that. He was wearing worn scuffed up blue jeans and a pair of dusty mustard colored work boots. He smelled good and sweaty, like he had just worked real hard out in the sun and heat, all fucking day. I picked up his tee shirt, sniffed it a few times and stuck it in my back pocket, leaving it hanging out and on display.

"A little souvenir," I said softly to Ronald, looking at the muscle boy's chest rising up and back down again as he slept his nipples the size of two pointy silver dollars on his chest. "My God, look at the tits on this kid. Real nice big control knobs for his dick I'll bet."

Ronald looked around the jobsite and took in the sight of the bags of quick drying cement and packaging rope strewn around the desolate place.

"I'm getting some real nasty ideas here Alex," Ronald said. "I think you may just get a lot more than this muscle boy's tee shirt as a souvenir."

As he spoke Ronald had placed one big hand atop the kid's head.

"Huhhhh, h-hey what, what are you dudes doin' here?" the muscle boy said as he opened his eyes, still more asleep than awake. "Y-you guys aren't supposed to be in here."

"Well, the welcome mat outside said otherwise muscle boy," Ronald said, leering down at the kid and curling a few fingers in his short hair.

With blinding speed Ronald yanked the muscle boy's head forward by his hair curled in his fingers and with the same speed thrust the kid's head back again...right against the concrete post he was sitting propped up against.

"Huuunnnfffff!!!" the muscle boy gasped as the back of his head connected with the concrete post.

"Holy fucks Ronald, that's a shitty ass thing to do to the poor kid," I said merrily.

"Huuuhhhhhh, wh-what do you mugs want here?" the muscle boy whimpered as Ronald meanly and forcefully yanked him to his booted feet by his hair. "AYYYYYY leggo of me man!!"

As the muscle boy was brought painfully to his feet his arms flailed out uselessly at his sides. Ronald yanked him a few feet away from the post and began spinning the kid in a clockwise direction, holding tightly to the handful of his hair.

"Huuuuhhhhhhhnnn, g-getting me dizzy here you fuck heads!!" the kid seethed.

"Ha, lookit him dance in his work boots Alex," Ronald mused, having a grand time spinning the kid like he was a top.

When the kid's butt spun past me I grabbed his red bandanna that was sticking out of the back pocket of his jeans.

"Huuuhhhhhhhh l-leggo of me man!!" the muscled construction worker grunted, angrily now.

"Sure thing kid," Ronald said, bent the kid over, pointed him at the concrete post and flung him forward.

"Ahhhhrrrrr God!!" the kid bellowed as he tottered helplessly toward the post, the top of his head connecting with it now. "Huuuuhhhhhhhhhnnnnn!!!"

His muscular arms involuntarily hugged the post as he slid to his knees.

"F-fuckers…" the muscle boy seethed in the stupor he'd been thrown into for the moment.

"Man, he's going to have some big lumps on his head by the time this little escapade is over," I said, holding up his red bandanna. "Although I think the sooner we get him gagged the better. We don't want this handsome muscle head attracting any unwanted attention while we have some fun with him in here."

"True story," Ronald said agreeably, pulling down the zipper on his jeans. "But before we cram that rag in his mouth lets make it taste really good for the kid."

Laughing meanly Ronald and I pissed a goodly amount of our yellow stream onto the muscle boy's already stinking and sweat soaked bandanna.

"F-fuckers, y-you guys ain't shovin' that thing in my mouth," the kid whimpered through clenched teeth, slowly getting to his feet, looking at Ronald and I with revenge in his eyes.

But before the weakened muscle boy could do anything Ronald again had him by a handful of his short hair.

"Looks like our new prize needs another tango lesson Alex," Ronald laughed and gave the muscle boy a hard punch to the old gut.

"Hoooofffffffff!!!" the kid sputtered and nearly jumped out of his boots as Ronald again spun him like a top around and around the dank large room, finally sending him flying against the post again.

This time the kid's back connected with the post and when he involuntarily threw his muscular arms behind the post to prevent himself from falling I took that opportunity to start getting him tied up good and tight to the post.

"H-hey, wh-what the fuck are you doin' man???" the kid seethed in disbelief as I used a good length of packaging rope to get him secured to the post, tying his upper muscular and succulent body real tight. "Just rob me and get it the fuck over with!!"

"Oh my dear muscle boy," Ronald said like a villain from an old time movie, holding the kid's piss soaked bandanna, right near his trembling lips. "We want a lot more than to just rob you."

That said Ronald crammed the bandanna deep into the now helpless muscle boy's mouth.

"RRRRRRMMMFFFF!!!" the kid sputtered and Ronald again clocked the back of his head against the post.

This time the kid's head lolled forward and spittle dripped from the sides of his gagged mouth. Ronald tied a length of rope over the bandanna, jamming it firmly in place.

"Man, how many lumps does that make for him?" I asked laughingly.

"Help me get his feet in that box over there," Ronald said. "When this kid comes around he's not going to believe the position he's in."

When the kid's head cleared he found himself tied to the post, his feet immured in the large box and his worn scuffed jeans down around his calves. His big cock and somewhat hairy balls were hanging out of the fly opening of his white under shorts. From the moment he came fully to he was in more than a rage as Ronald and I tweaked, squeezed, twisted, twirled, slurped, chewed and mauled his great big man tits...

"MMMFFFFFFF!!!" the muscle boy squealed as Ronald slurped and bit down on one of his man tits while I fingered and twisted the other one, my hand again wrapped around his big throbbing beefy manhood.

"Yeah, muscle boy wants to shoot that load don't you?" I chided him meanly. "Hates havin' two guys workin' him over like this, but you still want to get off don't you muscle boy?"

He huffed and snuffed at me, the scent of piss and sweat emanating from his gagged mouth. He nodded "yes" again, pleading with me with his eyes.

"Fuck man, I wouldn't be surprised if you were really enjoying all this shit we're heaping on you here muscle boy," I said and gave his cock a couple of strokes, but not enough to get him spurting his mess.

"HHHRRRRMMMFFF!!!" be cried out angrily as I let go of his cock again and Ronald and I went on teasing and squeezing his man tits with our fingers.

"Fuck it man, I could work this kid's nips all fucking day and night," Ronald said. "Too bad we got to get going soon to open the bar."

"Yeah, too bad we can't take muscle boy here with us and tie him up in the men's room," I said, giving one of his nipple tips a real hard twist.

"RRRRMMMFFFF!!!" the kid grunted looking up at the ceiling with his eyes squeezed shut.

"He would make a real nice decoration at the bar all roped up for everyone's use wouldn't you think Ronald?" I asked.

"Sure as shit man, sure as fucking shit," Ronald agreed.

I squeezed the muscle boy's nipple again at the same time that Ronald squeezed his other one. Glancing down I saw the kid's hardness twitch between his legs and his balls seemed to be throbbing. Pre cum oozed madly from his wide sexy slit.

"Damn, like I said, a guy's man tits are the control knobs for his dick," I said, giving the handsome construction dude a peck on the cheek.

A good hour later we finally stopped working the kid's nipples. All totaled we had been at it for a good two hours. By then they were swollen and worked up to the size of two over-ripe cherries on his succulent chest. His cock was enormous and hard between his muscular legs, his balls looked like they were chock filled with his thick mess of sperm and his nipples were bigger than two red ripe cherries on his exquisitely muscular chest.

"Well, from the look of things and in the interest of time I think we'd best be on our way Ronald," I said to my good buddy, hooking three fingers and my thumb around one of the muscle boy's sore nipples and jiggling it, looking at him lecherously. "Just want to thank you muscle boy for being so generous with your man tits and all."

I let go of his nipple as Ronald untied the ropes around the kid's upper body. I undid the rope around the piss soaked bandanna in his mouth and yanked it from his craw.

"Fuckers, perverts, *you'd best run after you get me untied you fuck heads!!*" the kid seethed as Ronald untied the ropes holding him to the post. "Mark my words man, this muscle boy is goin' to teach you two perverts a real hard lesson!!"

When the ropes fell away from his upper body and his arms were free we each took a few steps away from him.

"Come on Muscle boy, we're waitin' for our lesson!" Ronald chided the guy, goading him on as he bent down to get the box around his feet out of the way.

"Fucking pervs just got to get this box off my feet and then…" the kid started but then stopped in mid sentence. *"Holy fucking shit, no!!!"*

Looking down the kid saw that his big booted feet were encased in a bucket of solid cement up to his calves. His hard cock twitched mightily in front of him, droplets of pre cum oozing from his wide construction worker slit.

"Oh holy fucks, you bastards, you got my feet trapped in the quick drying cement," he blurted angrily at us.

"Here's a sledge hammer kid," Ronald said, tossing a rubber headed sledgehammer over to the trapped muscle boy.

The kid caught it, looking at us with eyes filled with revenge as we headed for the door of the job site. When we were outside we listened behind the closed door for the sounds of hammering. But at first what we heard was the sounds of the muscle boy panting and grunting as he jacked himself off a few times…

The Story of Lenny and Frank

(Two Executives Working Late)

My name is Frank; I work for a bank in New York City as an account manager for the bank's biggest and most top-notch customers and accounts. I'm thirty-eight years old and happily married. I have wavy brown hair, a neatly trimmed beard and mustache, and my eyes are green. I stand about five feet ten inches tall. The story I want to tell you about began about a year ago one night when I had gotten stuck working late. It was about six forty five PM and everyone had gone home for the day, everyone that was except for my boss Lenny and I. He was in his private office across the hall from mine, also working late. Earlier I had dropped off a report with him to look over and sign off on and I decided to go and pick it up to be filed away. Dressed in my black suit pants, a white shirt, red silk tie with matching suspenders, and black cap-toe shoes I walked out of my office and across the hall to Lenny's office. His door was halfway closed and I was able to hear him talking on the phone.

"Yeah, we're working on that deal for you now Marty." I heard Lenny saying to Marty (one of the bank's vice presidents.) "By this time next week we'll have that account and all the information that you'll need will be on your desk."

I knocked gently on his door and poked my head in. Lenny waved for me to come in. As I stepped into his office I saw that Lenny had his feet propped up on his desk and his shoes were off. He seemed very relaxed. He was wearing a white shirt, a colorful silk necktie, (colorful to match his personality) navy blue pinstriped trousers, and navy blue nylon dress socks. His shoes, I guessed, were on the floor under his desk. I stood in front of his desk as he continued talking on the phone. Lenny has brown straight hair pushed back from his forehead, crystal blue eyes, and he stands about five feet eight inches tall. He's the same age as I am.

"Sure Marty, I'll head up the meeting, no problem," Lenny said into the phone, looking at me and rolling his eyes.

I smiled at him and he held up a hand, indicating that I should wait a moment. I nodded politely. As he went on speaking to Marty he was wiggling his toes under his socks. It was then that I noticed the report I had come in for was under the heel of his foot. I saw that his signature (for approval) was at the bottom of the page. I pointed to the report and then pointed to the door, indicating that I would take the report and get on my way. Lenny pointed to his socked feet and smiled. Smiling back at him I placed my fingers and thumb tightly around his foot that was on my report and lifted it up off the desk. The musty scent of Lenny's day old socks wafted up to my nostrils, but I made no indication of it.

"Yeah okay Marty," Lenny said into the phone as I held his foot up with one hand and took my report with my other hand.

Did I feel awkward holding my boss' socked foot in my hand? I sure as shit did. I lowered Lenny's foot back to the desk and turned to leave his office.

"Hold one second Marty, please," Lenny said and covered the mouthpiece of the phone with the palm of his hand. "Uh Frank, could you wait a minute?"

I turned around and faced him.

"Have a seat Frank," he said to me, pointing to the chair in front of his desk.

I sat down and then Lenny's socked feet were staring me in the face.

"Yeah that's Frank whose here Marty," Lenny said into the phone. "My right hand man, Frank."

I smiled and then for some reason I found myself staring intently at Lenny's socked feet propped comfortably up on his desk. His feet were actually exquisitely shaped, perfect arches, big round heels, and through his thin dress socks I could tell he had big toes. They were outlined perfectly because of the way his socks were clinging to his sweaty feet. The smell of his foot sweat again filled my nostrils. I was sure that he noticed me looking intently at his feet as he still went on talking to Marty. I nonchalantly placed my hand over my mouth and nose, (the hand that I had used to lift Lenny's foot off his desk a few moments ago) trying to pretend that I had an itch. I sniffed my hand and it smelled slightly like Lenny's foot sweat. As I lowered my hand I saw Lenny looking at me intently.

"Okay Marty, I better get going myself," Lenny said into the phone. "I have to finish up here and then get home."

He told Marty to have a good night and then he hung up the phone. With his feet still propped up on the desk he leaned back in his chair and looked at me, smiling from ear to ear.

"That was some statistics report Frank," Lenny said to me, pointing at the paper I was holding.

"Thanks Lenny," I replied happily but nervously. "I'm glad you approved of it."

For whatever the reason I felt tension in the air, not scary tension but another kind that I could not put a name to.

"Are you in a rush Frank?" he asked me, wiggling his toes under his thin blue nylon socks.

"Er, no, not really," I said nervously, stealing glances at his socked feet. "Why do you ask?"

I was suddenly able to *really* smell the odor from Lenny's socked feet from where I was sitting.

"I couldn't help but notice how you smelled your hand after you had lifted my foot off the desk a few minutes ago," Lenny said, still smiling and still wiggling his big toes under his socks. "You maybe got a thing for feet or something?"

"I-uh-I," I started to say, not knowing what the hell I was going to say.

It's not every-day that a guy's boss asks him if he has a foot fetish. Actually I had never had a foot fetish; at least I didn't think that I did. That is until I saw Lenny's exquisitely shaped socked feet resting atop his desk that evening.

"It's okay guy, a lot of people like feet," Lenny went on, wiggling those big toes of his under his socks. "It's just that most people don't talk about it. I love having my wife *or anyone* for that matter massage my tired feet for me at the end of the day. The only problem is that my wife says my feet stink at the end of the day."

We smiled at each other across the desk. His wife wasn't lying, Lenny's feet sure as fuck did stink. But yet I could not tear myself away. Actually, I could not believe that my direct manager was saying these things to me. But I somehow found it to be exciting in a strange way…

"So what do you say Frank?" Lenny asked me, sounding seductive yet macho at the same time.

I put the report I was holding down on his desk, leaned forward, and wrapped my trembling hands around one of Lenny's feet. I began massaging it, kneading it, and digging my thumbs gently into the meaty bottom of it.

"Ahhh, that's nice Frank," Lenny said, leaning back in his chair and relaxing.

As I massaged his smelly, socked foot something began to happen that I could not believe. My dick began to get hard in my suit pants. I was never one for being a foot freak but *there was something about that.* Something about Lenny's feet was driving me wild. Maybe it was the fact that even though we were friends he was also my boss. Maybe it was his power over me that was driving me wild as I massaged his foot. I moved my hands over to his other foot and began massaging that one next. Lenny sighed contentedly. The smell of his foot odor was assaulting my nose and instead of pulling away from it I found myself moving closer to it, being drawn to it like a magnet so to speak. As I continued massaging his foot I leaned forward even more and pressed my nose against his socked toes. I inhaled deeply.

"How does it smell Frank?" Lenny asked me.

"Like foot sweat," I replied. "Musty, sweaty,"

"Shit man, I've been wearing those damned socks since six AM Frankie boy," Lenny told me. "Do you expect them to smell fresh?"

"No," I replied with my nose against his foot.

I took my hands off his foot and daringly stuck out my tongue. I licked the bottom of Lenny's foot. I could not believe I was doing it but I actually licked his stinking socked foot. Lenny smiled broadly, smiling as if he had just closed a major business deal. I licked his foot some more.

"I don't believe this Frankie boy," Lenny said to me. "I expected to perhaps get a foot rub, but not a foot licking."

I ran the tip of my tongue over the side of his foot, over the arch, (God I loved his arches) and down the other side. I repeated that a few times and Lenny seemed to be thoroughly enjoying it.

"Ohhh yeah Frankie boy, lick my socks," Lenny said happily. "Clean 'em up good for me."

He had never called me Frankie boy before. There was something romantic yet authoritative about it. I didn't seem to mind at all though, as long as he allowed me to lick those feet of his. I continued licking his warm musty socked foot. I licked the sides of it some more and then leaned forward more and ran the tip of my tongue over the top of his foot, flicking my tongue over those big toes of his, pushing his pants leg up and out of the way. I wanted to really get at Lenny's socks.

"Man oh man, what would your wife Nancy say if she could see you now?" Lenny asked me.

"Oh yeah? What would your wife Grace say if she could see you now?" I asked him and immediately resumed licking his socked foot.

I was leaning over Lenny's desk in full now, licking and smelling his foot. I drooled over the top of his foot and then sucked up my saliva. I moved my mouth over the top of his foot and licked and kissed his toes under his socks.

"Kiss 'em Frank," Lenny whispered to me. "Kiss my toes."

I did as he told me to do kissing each of his toes a few times each. Then, I sucked on his toes through his socks and kissed each of them a few times each all over again. Lenny watched with total satisfaction. When his sock was cleaned on the first foot I moved over to his other foot and eagerly began licking that one.

"Shit, *you really are enjoying this Frankie boy,"* Lenny said to me. "I am going to have the cleanest socks when I get home tonight. Grace isn't going to believe it when she does the wash."

As he spoke my dick grew harder in my pants. Lenny folded his arms over his chest and watched as I ran my tongue over his toes. I didn't forget to kiss them a few times each.

"Shit, what a foot freak I have here," Lenny mused. "I'm getting some real big ideas Frankie boy. We are going to have lots of fun with all this."

When I was done with his other foot I stopped licking it and stood up straight behind his desk.

"I, uh, think your socks are all clean now Lenny," I said to him, not believing what I had just done, yet wanting to do it again and again.

Lenny looked his feet over and then looked up at me. He saw the hard bulge in my trousers and smiled from ear to ear.

"Holy shit Frankie boy, *you really did enjoy all that foot licking didn't you?"* he asked me. "Just look at that fucking boner in your suit pants."

Standing there practically at attention I took a deep breath.

"Tell you what Frankie boy, why don't you get a little comfortable and then I'll let you service my feet again, *bare this time*," Lenny said suggestively.

Lenny moved his feet off his desk, pulled his socks off, and dropped them on his desk.

"G-get comfortable?" I asked him, not knowing what he meant.

"Sure, take off that shirt and tie, the suspenders, *the suit pants, relax*," Lenny said to me. "You can kneel down over here on my side of the desk and clean up my stinky feet for me.

Before I knew what the fuck I was doing I found myself undoing the Windsor knot in my necktie.

"That's it Frank," Lenny said to me, crossing one of his bare feet over his knee.

As I took off my shirt I looked at his socks lying on his desk.

"You enjoyed licking those socks of mine eh Frankie boy?" he asked me snidely.

"Yeah, I suppose I did at that," I replied nervously.

"Tell you what, you let me do what I want with you, you lick my bare feet till they smell real good, and I'll put my socks back on so you can have the pleasure of licking them all over again. Deal?"

"Sure Lenny, deal," I said anxiously and slipped my suspenders off my unbuttoned shirt.

I felt as if I was in a trance as I put my shirt, tie, and suspenders down on the chair behind Lenny's desk and then proceeded to unbutton my pants. I took my pants off over my Florsheim cap-toes and socks. Moments later I was wearing just my frosty white BVD briefs, my black cap-toe shoes, and my sheer black calf length dress socks. I was now standing on the other side of Lenny's desk. Unbelievably he had tied my hands behind me with some packaging rope that he had in his desk. Also unbelievably I didn't protest in the least when he had told me to stand still with my back to him and my wrists crossed behind me. As he roped my hands behind me my dick grew still harder in my briefs. Pre cum oozed through the cotton material of my briefs and I took a deep breath. Lenny said that it was for my own good that he'd tied my hands behind me, as he didn't want me touching my hard-on while I was busy servicing his bare feet. I was to concentrate on the task at hand, or to be more precise, I was to concentrate on the task at foot. As I stood there while he roped my hands behind me I agreed totally with what he said. More than anything at that moment I really wanted to be busy licking his feet. Fuck, I would have let him rope me up from head to toe just to get at those feet of his.

"So, are you ready to lick and suck my smelly bare feet?" Lenny asked me as he turned me around facing him.

When he reached up and ran a finger through my chest hair my breath caught in my throat.

"*I'm ready,* " I whispered breathlessly.

"I can see that," he said and patted the pre cumming hard-on in my briefs. "Get down on your knees Frankie boy."

Again I did as he said and hastily pressed my nose against his foot that was on his knee. It really did stink, but I stuck out my tongue and began licking the side of it, paying special attention to the arch really swirling my tongue over it.

"Ahhhh yeah, feels great Frank," Lenny said contentedly. "Lick my foot."

He ran his fingers through my hair, squeezed the back of my neck, and then leaned back in his chair as I serviced his foot. I licked the sides of his foot up and down and licked the bottom of it a few times. The flesh on the bottom of Lenny's foot was soft and meaty. I sucked at it a few times and then licked it some more. I could not believe any of this. I mean, there I was, a big deal executive, stripped to my briefs, shoes, and socks, *and* on my damned knees with my hands roped behind me, licking my boss' stinking bare foot. As I licked Lenny's foot he reached for his phone.

"I'd better call Grace and tell her that I'm going to be a little later than expected," Lenny said.

"Yeah, I'd better call Nancy as well, now that you mention it," I said, looking up at him, drool all over my lips and chin.

"I'll call her for you Frankie boy," Lenny said as he dialed his home telephone number. "You just get busy sucking my toes and licking in between them too. Lots of cheesy treats for you there."

I did as he said and he put the receiver to his ear. I began sucking his big toe, swirling my tongue around it at the same time.

"Hi Grace, it's me," Lenny said into the phone. "Listen honey, I'm going to be here a little later than I expected. I'm working on a project with Frank."

He paused to listen as she spoke.

"Another hour or so at least I would think," he said, grinning down at me as I sucked his toe like crazy. "Okay? Love you babe."

He hung up the phone and smiled down at me.

"Now for your wife," he said as he picked up the receiver and dialed my home number.

As he dialed I was busy licking between his first two toes, cleaning all the sweat and grunge out of them. He placed the receiver to his ear again.

"Hi Nancy, its Lenny," he said as my wife answered the phone. "How are you?"

He paused as she replied.

"Frank asked me to call you and tell you that we're working on a project here and that he'll be a little later than expected," he said to my wife. "He got a little tied up in his work and I'm trying to help him out."

I nearly gulped as he said that, but instead wrapped my lips around two of his toes. I began sucking them.

"Okay Nancy, talk to you soon," Lenny said to my wife. "Bye now."

He hung up the phone and leaned back in his chair.

"Okay Frankie boy, hurry up and finish with those rancid toes of mine and then you can get to work on my other bare foot," Lenny said teasingly. "And I assure you, it's going to taste just as funky as the one you're working now."

As I sucked Lenny's toes he picked up his socks from the desk and sniffed them.

"Ahhh, nice and fresh," he murmured.

When I finished with his first bare foot he moved it down on the floor and crossed his other foot over his other knee in front of my face. I instantly got busy. As I licked his other raunchy smelling foot my dick pounded long and hard in my briefs, aching for release.

"Ahhhh, yeah, feels fucking great," Lenny crooned. "I should have you do this for me all the time Frankie boy. Just think about it, having you in here, tied up, licking and servicing my damned smelly feet all the fucking time."

My heart pounded hard as he said that. The thought of constantly licking Lenny's feet with or without his socks on them seemed to be driving me wild. To show my joy I speedily licked his foot all over, sucked his toes, and licked in between those stinking toes. When I was done I stayed on my knees as Lenny inspected my work. He seemed to approve of his now very clean feet.

"Stand up Frankie boy," Lenny said.

I pulled myself to my feet as Lenny rolled his socks back onto his feet. He looked up at me and placed his hands on my hips, his thumbs in the sides of my BVD's.

"No one will ever have to know about any of this Frankie boy," he said to me, squeezing my hips as he kept his thumbs tucked in the sides of my briefs.

"No sir, I was actually hoping you would say that," I replied, already looking down at his socked feet, my mouth drooling.

Lenny stood up and stepped behind me. He grabbed my upper arms and pulled me close to himself.

"Anxious to lick my socks again huh Frankie boy?" he asked me, sounding lustful, his lips just grazing the short hairs on the back of my neck.

"Y-yeah, I guess so," I replied breathlessly.

Actually, I was dying to be licking his socks again. He let go of my arms and stepped in front of me, looking down at my feet.

"What about those sheer socks of yours Frankie boy?" Lenny asked me. "Do they need cleaning?"

"I-I would suppose so sir," I said. "I mean, like you I've been wearing my socks since six AM."

"Good, when you're done licking my socks all over again I'll put your socks on my feet and you can lick them clean too," Lenny said and sat down in his desk chair. "I sure as shit do love the way that tongue of yours feels as it glides over my feet Frankie boy."

And I thought he was going to volunteer to lick my socked feet. No way though, Lenny was the boss after all.

"In that case you'd better call our wives again," I said as he propped his socked feet up on the desk for me.

"Why?" he asked.

"Because my socks are going to need *a real good cleaning,* " I said jokingly.

We both laughed and Lenny told me to get busy licking his socks again. This time I began by sucking his toes through the thin nylon material.

"Ohhhhh yeah, feels so fucking good Frankie boy," Lenny said to me.

We finally left the office an hour and a half later; both of us with licked clean socks on our feet and hard fucking dicks in our suit pants...

The day after I had licked Lenny's socks and feet I was at my desk working on one of my accounts when my phone rang.

"Hello, Frank speaking," I said into the receiver.

"Frankie boy, it's Lenny," Lenny said to me. "What say you come into my office and spend lunch hour with me. We can talk about that problem that has you all tied up in knots."

I could actually feel him smiling from ear to ear as I gulped hard and looked up at the clock. It was five minutes to twelve.

"N-now Lenny?" I asked him nervously.

"Sure, why not?" he asked me and hung up the phone.

I hung up my phone and stood up. Dressed that day in a blue suit, white shirt, patterned silk necktie, black lace-up wing tips, and black nylon ribbed calf length dress socks I walked across the hall to Lenny's office. I knocked twice and walked in. He was sitting at his desk, looking pretty relaxed.

"Come on in Frank, relax," he said to me. "You look jumpier than a long tailed cat in a room filled with rocking chairs."

I smiled, locked the door, and sat down across from him.

"Feeling okay?" he asked me.

"Yeah, fine," I replied, wishing that his feet were propped up on the desk.

I had seen him come in to work that morning and like me he was wearing black lace-up wing tips. I wanted so much to get my mouth on his feet again. When I had arrived home the night before it was all I could think about. As I drifted off to sleep I thought about licking Lenny's feet. Yeah, I wanted to get my mouth all over Lenny's feet again. But at the moment he had other plans for me.

"Did you have sex with Nancy last night?" he asked me point blank.

"I-uh, no," I replied. "As a matter of fact I didn't."

"I didn't have sex either last night," he said to me and smiled big and wide. "Looks like we both have a lot of executive spunk all stored up and waiting for release eh Frankie boy?"

"Er-yeah, I guess so," I said to him, not knowing yet just what he had in mind.

"What say we do something about that Frankie boy?" Lenny asked me.

"Wh-what do you have in mind Lenny?" I asked him nervously.

He smiled and gestured for me to stand up. I did as he instructed. My dick was already hard in my pants.

"Get that shirt and tie off Frankie boy, and let me get your hands roped behind you," Lenny said with an air of authority in his voice. "Then I'll tell you *exactly* what I have in mind."

As I reached for the knot in my tie Lenny took the rope out of his desk. Without a word I undid my tie and took off my shirt. Lenny came over to me with the rope and ran his hand over my very hairy chest. He pushed tufts of hair out of the way of my big pink nipples and squeezed them hard a few times each.

"Ohhhhh," I moaned softly and contentedly.

"Nice tits," Lenny commented and then turned me around with my back to him.

I hung my head down and breathed slowly as he tied my hands behind me.

"L-Lenny," I said breathlessly.

"Yeah Frank?" he replied.

"Wh-what does all this make us?" I asked him as he wound the rope tightly around my wrists.

"Very daring and adventurous Frank," he said. "All this makes us two very daring and adventurous men."

He finished tying my hands and gave my butt a slap. I turned back around facing him. He again ran a hand over my hairy chest.

"Damn Frank, you're bushier than a bear," Lenny said as he played with my chest hairs.

Then, to my surprise he leaned down and gave one of my nipples a few hearty sucks, holding it tightly between his front teeth.

"Ohhhhhrrrr fuck, Lenny," I moaned.

"Tastes good Frankie boy, real nice tits you got here," Lenny said and took me by my upper arm.

He walked me behind his desk and sat down in his chair. He crossed his leg and I saw that he was wearing black nylon dress socks. My mouth filled with drool as I looked at his feet.

"Want to lick my dress socked feet huh?" Lenny asked me, knowing all too well that I wanted to.

"Ohhhh yeah," I replied breathlessly.

"Just like last night eh Frankie boy?" he teased me.

"Yes sir, just like last night," I said to him, my hairy chest heaving up and down with each breath I took.

"Damn, I love seeing you beg Frank," Lenny said with satisfaction. "I knew last night that I could bring out the foot freak in you. I guess there really is something about a guy in a pair of dark colored dress socks."

That said he laid his foot across his knee and teasingly snapped his sock against his leg.

"Please Lenny," I pleaded.

Now I knew why he insisted on tying my hands behind me.

"Get under my desk Frankie boy," Lenny ordered me. "That's where you'll stay for the rest of the day."

"But, what about my work?" I asked him, not protesting in the least about being hunkered under his desk with his musty scented feet nearby all afternoon.

"I'll tell everyone you went home early," Lenny responded. "I'll tell them you weren't feeling well."

I squatted down on my haunches and made my way under Lenny's big desk. I settled into a kneeling position, my face right by his crotch, his dick was hard in his suit pants.

"Comfortable under there Frankie boy?" Lenny asked me as he slid his chair in close to me.

"Yeah, I suppose so," I said and pressed my mouth against his crotch. "Now I know why you wanted me under here."

"Shit, didn't even have to tell you to get on my crotch," Lenny quipped.

He unzipped his pants and his big dick flopped out, long, beefy and hard. With no hesitation I took it in my mouth and sucked it. Lenny wrapped his legs around my body as I milked him.

"Ohhhh yeah, now I've made you into a cock sucker Frankie boy," Lenny panted.

"I'll suck you off Lenny and I'll stay under this desk all fucking day *as long as I get your feet later on*," I said and took his dick back in my mouth again. "Even though I'm the one tied up down here and even though you are my boss that is my condition, I want your feet..."

"Deal Frankie boy, fucking deal," Lenny replied breathlessly to my proposal.

With his legs wrapped tightly around me I sucked him and sucked him. His dick was pulsing and hot in my mouth. I poked my tongue into his piss slit a few times. That really got him gasping let me tell you. When he came the first time I didn't hesitate to swallow every drop of his executive spunk. He ground the heels of his shoes against my sides as I chugged down his juices.

"Oh yeah Frankie boy, lunch is served," Lenny said to me as he shot his load. "Lunch is fucking served."

During the afternoon while Lenny was out of the office in a meeting he kept me stashed under his desk. To make sure I didn't go anywhere he roped my feet together and gagged me. He locked his office door and kept his desk chair pushed in. My shirt and tie he locked in his desk and I stayed under that desk, sweating as my dick pounded long and hard in my pants. When Lenny returned a while later from the meeting he sat down behind his desk, reached under it and pulled the gag off me, and without a word had his dick out of his pants again. I knelt there under his desk and slurped his meat into my mouth again. By evening Lenny was just finishing up his work for the day. He now had me standing next to him as he signed off on reports and other stuff. I stood there stripped to my shoes, socks, and briefs, standing practically at attention, waiting for Lenny to get to me. My hands were still tied behind me but my feet were untied. My gag was hanging loosely around my neck. When Lenny finally took off his shoes and propped his socked feet up on the desk he smiled up at me, signaling that it was time. I instantly leaned over the desk and began licking his feet. They smelled and tasted totally raunchy. I had become my boss' foot slave and there would be no turning back, ever.

A Boner Book

A Party after the Ball Game

The game was over and my team had won. Again we had won. *And it was because of me that we had won.* I was in the locker room with my two best college buddies Rocky and Mark. I was wearing just the dirty pants of my baseball uniform and my filthy white sweat socks, which were pushed down around my ankles. I was sitting on a bench with my back against the lockers as Rocky and Mark sat at my sides, sucking, slurping, and licking my nipples like crazy. I was in total ecstasy as they slurped heartily on my big nipples like crazy, chewing on them, biting them, and fucking eating them. I was sweating like mad and I smelled pretty ripe because I had not yet showered since the game was over. I wanted my two best buddies to really enjoy what they were doing to me at the moment.

"Ohhhh yeahhh feels so good," I whispered my dick long and hard in my baseball uniform pants.

Rocky and Mark were servicing my nipples because of a dare I had presented to them during the game.

My name is Cliff Stevens, I'm twenty-one years old, and I'm the star player on Brooklyn College's baseball team. I was born and raised in Brooklyn New York and when I had to decide on which college to attend Brooklyn College seemed like the only logical choice. I have blond hair, blue eyes, I stand five feet ten inches tall, and I'm pretty lean and muscular from participating in sports a lot of the time. My body is hairless and smooth. During the game we had just won I had told Rocky and Mark that I was going to hit a homerun when I got up to bat. Rocky said it would never happen, smirking at me as he said it. I had hit two homeruns in our last game and he didn't think lightning would strike in the same place twice. I insisted that I would hit a homerun *and* win us the game. Mark came over to us in the dugout, gave the back of my neck a squeeze, and said that if I hit a homerun he would suck one of my big tits. We all laughed heartily at his remark, being that my buddies had always chided me on what big nipples I have for a guy.

"And I'll fuckin' suck the other one," Rocky said gleefully.

I looked at the two of them and with a look of outright determination on my face I told them that they were on. If I hit a homerun and won our team the game Rocky and Mark would have to suck my nipples, before I showered. I told them I wanted them to smell and taste all the raunch on me after a hard game. They said I was on, confident that I would not hit a homerun. Actually I think they wanted me to hit a homerun. I think they wanted to have at my tits. And God knew, and I knew, just how good it felt to have one's tits sucked and slurped on…and there were those of us who didn't give a flying fuck whether it was a girl or two working your tits or a couple of your male teammates. So, with a smirk on my face I picked up my bat and walked out onto the filed when my name was announced. What I didn't know at the time was what my two buddies were planning for me for later on. Needless to say I hit a homerun and won the game for my team. Rocky and Mark came charging over to me, hoisted me to their shoulders, and carried me off the field amid the cheers and applause of the crowd and the rest of our team. I waved my arms triumphantly as I was carried off the field, hero style. They carried me all the way into the locker room where I received pats on the back, pats on the ass, and a lot of congratulations. While most of the team showered and then got dressed Rocky, Mark, and I held back, waiting for everyone to leave the locker room.

"I hope you two are ready to fulfill your end of the dare," I said to them as I pulled off my sweat soaked team shirt. "My tits sure are in need of some serious attention."

I ran my hands over my large brown tits and I saw that Rocky and Mark were actually looking at them hungrily.

"Shit, your tits look better than my girlfriend's," Rocky said and licked his lips.

"Yeah man, how'd you get such fucking sexy tits?" Mark teased me and squeezed one of them, sending a searing chill through me.

I sat down on the bench in front of my locker and took off my sneakers. My sweat sock scent assaulted our nostrils. My feet, my armpits, and my chest were all drenched in sweat, making me smell real fucking ripe for my two good buddies. After a while we were the last three in the locker room. Rocky and Mark stripped down to their underpants and sat down at my sides.

"Ready?" Mark a big burly guy with brown hair, brown eyes, and a muscular body asked, giving one of my nipples a hard squeeze, sending another chill through my very being.

"Let's do it," Rocky, a guy with black hair, blue eyes, and kind of stocky but muscular replied. "We said we would."

They both leaned down and slurped one of my nipples each into their mouths.

"Ohhhhh shit, yeah, oh fuckin' A," I crooned. "That feels great guys. Work those fucking sexy tits of mine."

I stretched my legs out in front of myself, leaned my head back against the lockers, closed my eyes, and basked in the ecstasy I was in.

"Ooooo yeah," I said breathlessly as they worked my nipples. "Fuckin' suck on those tits."

Rocky and Mark teased the tips of my tits with their tongues and sucked them more and more and more, running their big hands over my sweaty mid section. My dick was hard as a rock in my uniform pants and as soon as my two buddies were done with my tits I would jerk off in the shower to relieve myself, or so I thought. My two good buddies had other plans for me, as I would soon find out. I placed my hands behind their big necks and tousled their sweaty hair.

"Man, we all smell like pure raunch," I said jokingly.

Rocky and Mark each kissed my nipples.

"Hey guys, no kissin' here," I said. "We ain't faggots after all. This is just plain ol' guy's fun."

"Sure is," Rocky murmured, kissed my tit again, and sucked it back into his mouth.

"Ohhhhh yeah," I moaned, not commenting on the fact that he had just kissed my tit again.

When they stopped a little while later my tits were erect and slightly swollen. My two buddies sat close to me, running their hands over my mid-section, giving my erect tits a few stolen squeezes.

"So, are you satisfied?" Rocky asked me. "We sucked your damned sexy but smelly tits."

"Yeah, I'm satisfied," I replied with a smile. "Got a good fucking boner in my pants that I'm going to work on in the shower."

Rocky and Mark smiled at each other across me.

"You know Cliff, we're going to a party at my friend Dennis' house after we're done here," Rocky said to me. "You may want to join us. What do you say?"

"I don't know," I began.

"Come on Cliff, it'll be fun," Mark said insistently.

"Okay," I said. "I just need to shower, and so do you guys."

"You won't need to shower Cliff," Rocky said. "*You* can go as you are."

"What do you mean?" I asked him curiously. "I smell like a fucking toilet."

Suddenly, my two buddies grabbed me tightly by my arms and yanked me roughly to my feet.

"Hey!!!" I yelped. "What the fuck are you two up to?"

Holding my arms tightly behind me they walked me over to Rocky's locker, which was standing open. At the bottom of the locker I saw a pile of rope and some of Rocky's dirty and smelly sweat socks.

"Oh fuck, *no,* " I said desperately.

"You made us suck those damned smelly tits of yours Cliffy boy," Rocky said meanly. "Now it's payback time."

"Yeah, and we promised Dennis that we would bring a surprise to his party," Mark said. *"Surprise Cliff!"*

"No, no!!!" I yelled and struggled in their grasps.

Mark, being the more muscular of the two guys held me tightly by both arms as Rocky bent down to get some rope from his locker.

"Hands behind you Cliffy boy," Rocky said mockingly.

Moments later I was lying on the floor on my stomach with my hands tied tightly behind me and my feet tied together, pulled up behind me and tied to my hands. I was in what is known as a hog-tied position. I was gagged with one of Rocky's awful tasting and overly used sweat socks with another sock tied over it, jamming it firmly in place.

"RRRRmmmffff!!!" I sputtered angrily.

I squirmed helplessly on the floor while Rocky and Mark showered, taking their time. I heard them laughing about what a splash I was going to make at the party. Rocky said he couldn't wait to see the expression on Dennis' face when they showed up with me all tied up.

"Fuck, we'll let everyone at the party suck and slurp his big sexy tits," Mark guffawed. "Seeing as he likes having them worked on so much."

I was sweating with fear and anger. My two best buddies, *right!!!* When Rocky and Mark were done in the shower they dried off and got dressed. I watched them helplessly from the floor, looking up at them in anger.

"Relax Cliff, you're going to love the party," Rocky said as he pulled on clean white sweat socks.

"Hhhhrrrmmmmmmfff!!!" I sputtered as I struggled like mad to get myself untied.

Rocky and Mark laughed hysterically. When they were done getting dressed they squatted over me, untied my feet, (leaving my hands tied behind me) and turned me over onto my back. I looked up at them helplessly as they ran their hands over my chest. It was matted with sweat and stinking.

"What say we have one more go at these tits of his before we get going?" Rocky asked Mark. "His fucking nubs are better than my girlfriend's."

"Sure thing," Mark said. "And I have *another idea.*"

I panicked when Mark placed his hand over my crotch.

"Fucking Cliffy boy is hard as his baseball bat man," Mark said gleefully. "I'm going to jack him off so he'll smell even better later on."

"Mmmmmfff..." I sputtered as they each started sucking and slurping one of my nipples each again.

Saliva dripped from the sides of my gagged mouth and I was now sweating all over. I smelled pretty bad, even to myself. They sucked my nipples hard till they were beyond sore and when they stopped sucking them they were all red, swollen, and pointy. They gave them a few nasty squeezes and twists, causing me to scream in pain into my sock gag. As I looked down at my sore nipples the thought of a house full of party people taking turns sucking them sent me into an angry frenzy. My poor nipples would be more than beyond sore if this happened. But alas, I was powerless to stop it from happening. Mark unzipped my baseball uniform pants, reached in, and brought out my fear-hard and pulsing dick.

"Man, what a piece of meat he has!!" Rocky said as Mark began slowly stroking my big juicy dick. "Guy must be at least nine fucking inches or more."

"And thick," Mark said, stroking me faster. "Real fucking thick."

It didn't take long for me to shoot a big load of jock spunk all over my chest, my nipples, my stomach area, and onto my pants.

"*RRRRmmmfffff!!!*" I roared mightily as I shot my load, squirming on the floor. "Mmmmmfff!!!"

My body shook and trembled in ecstasy as Mark stroked me and stroked me, even after I was done, forcing every drop out of my piss hole. When I was finally done he let go of my dick and packed it back into my pants as Rocky smeared my cum all over my chest, my nipples, (squeezing them hard as he did so) and stomach region with his fingers.

"Hot load Cliff," Rocky said mockingly. "Maybe someone at the party will get you off again too."

"Oh I can guarantee that," Mark said. "Now, let's shoot our loads, all over him of course, and then we'll be on our way."

My two buddies stood up over me, pulled their big dicks out of their jeans, and began stroking themselves.

"Mmmmffff!!!" I sputtered angrily at them.

Fucking bastards were going to cum all over me. And sure enough they both shot a giant load of soup each, all over my chest, stomach, and pants, adding to my mess. After they were packed back into their jeans they re-tied my feet and hauled me up to their shoulders. When they carried me over their shoulders out of the locker room and to their van which was parked behind the baseball field I smelled a little more than ripe. This time I was not glad that my two buddies were carrying me off, this time there was no crowd cheering for me. *This time I was being kidnapped!*

"RRRRmmmmffff!!!" I roared madly.

They tossed me into the back of their van, (I honestly don't know which of them owned the van) blindfolded me, and slammed the back doors shut.

"Rastards!!!" I screamed in a muffled gagged tone of voice.

The van started moving and I was on my way to the party at their friend Dennis' house. As the van moved through the Brooklyn streets I tried again to get myself untied but it was useless. I was tied too tight. The taste of Rocky's sweat sock in my mouth was rancid and I swore to myself like a sailor every time I swallowed his foot sweat. When the van stopped a little while later I heard Rocky and Mark get out. The back doors opened and they hauled me roughly out. They stood me up on the ground and untied my feet, leaving my hands tied behind me.

"With all the cars that are parked out here it looks like everyone is here already," Rocky said to Mark.

"Ready to have those big titties of yours worked on all night Cliffy boy?" Mark asked me and squeezed one of my nipples hard.

"RRRRmmmmfff!!!" I wailed miserably.

Holding me by my arms they walked me to the door of Dennis' house and rang the bell. When Dennis opened the door Rocky took the blindfold off me.

"Hey you guys, well, well, what do we have here?" Dennis asked, taking in the unusual scene before him.

I recognized Dennis from the Brooklyn College campus. He was blond like me, but taller and more muscular looking.

"We promised you a surprise Dennis," Mark said. "And you probably thought that we were going to bring a bottle of wine."

All three of the college guys laughed heartily as my eyes spun in disbelief in my head. I then noticed that Dennis was looking at me hungrily.

"This is Cliff Stevens," Rocky said to Dennis. "He's the star player on the college team. He's the guy who hit the homerun that won us the game today."

Dennis smirked meanly.

"Why is he all tied up and gagged?" Dennis asked, his smirk turning into a smile. "And why the fuck do his tits look all raw? What have you two jokers been up to this time?"

"We'll tell you inside," Mark said, pushing me over to Dennis.

"Fine with me," Dennis said, taking me by my upper arm. "Come on Hot shot; let's find some champagne to pour over you in honor of your winning homerun. Fucking guys, kidnap a hot shot baseball player for me."

"Mmmmffff!!!" I said miserably as Dennis walked me into the crowded house, Rocky and Mark following closely behind.

"Everybody!!" Dennis called out, holding me tightly by both upper arms now. "This handsome bound and gagged young stud is Cliff Stevens. He is the star player on the Brooklyn College baseball team, but for tonight he is ours for the party, to do with what we please."

The party consisted of all young college guys. At the sight of me they all hooted and hollered loudly, applauding too. I was able to see that most of them were already semi lit with drink. I recognized some of them from the Brooklyn College campus. My heart thundered when I recognized some of them from the opposing college team we had beaten today.

"He likes to have his tits tortured!!" Rocky yelled out and I turned and looked at him in total anger.

All the men applauded more loudly, (men love tits) yelling things like "Give him to me!! Or "C'mere Hot thing let me suck your big girly tits!!" What a night I was in for. I again turned and looked at Rocky and Mark angrily.

"Okay, seeing as I'm the host of this shindig I get first crack at this hot baseball player," Dennis said.

He let go of my arms and in a fast move had me slung over one of his shoulders like a sack of potatoes, his hand pressing hard against my butt. Everyone cheered and laughed as Dennis carried me toward a private room.

"RRRRRmmmfff!!!" I roared madly.

In a small bedroom Dennis put me down on my socked feet and looked me over.

"You really are a hot looking guy Cliffy," he mused and grabbed me by my butt cheeks, chomping down hard on one of my sore nipples.

"Mmmmmffff!!!" I wailed in pain as Dennis chewed hard on the nipple he had in his mouth. "Mmmmmfff!!!"

I struggled hard to pull away from him but he was strong as an ox. His hands moved inside the back of my baseball uniform pants, and he squeezed my butt cheeks harder, kneading them. Unbelievably, my dick was hard as a rock in my pants. Actually, it had been hard since Rocky and Mark had carried me out of the locker room and to their van. Dennis suckled my nipple like a nursing baby, driving me batty, swirled his tongue over it and drove me crazy with a mixture of pain and pleasure. He grabbed my butt cheeks tighter and hoisted me a few inches off the floor.

"Hrrrrrummmffff!!!" I cried out as my feet left the floor.

Dennis stopped sucking my nipple and looked at me with a big wicked smile.

"I bet that sock tastes real good huh Cliffy boy?" he asked me, rubbing me against himself erotically. "Is that one of Rocky's sweat socks?"

I nodded that it was a look of agony in my eyes.

"Fucking guy's foot sweat could knock out a boxer," Dennis said and gave each of my nipples a kiss. "And the fucking guy crams one of those stinkers into your mouth. But I bet it tastes real fucking good."

He put me down on the floor and got a bottle of champagne out from under the bed. He opened the bottle and poured the champagne over my head. In moments my hair was soaked with champagne and it dripped down my chest and onto my pants. Dennis licked as much of the champagne off my chest as possible, paying special attention to what had landed on my poor nipples. When he was done slurping the champagne off me he placed a hand over my crotch.

"Fuckin' hard as a rock in there," Dennis laughed. "Looks to me like you're enjoying all this shit."

I nodded no as he stroked my dick through my pants and with my eyes I pleaded with him to stop. I was about to cream in my pants.

"Mmmmfff..." I moaned.

"Oh yeah, never thought I would get to jack off a hot baseball player Cliffy boy," Dennis mused and gave one of my nipples a lick.

Then, a few minutes later I shot my second load, right into my baseball uniform pants.

"Rrrrrmmmfff!!!" I cried out. "MMMmmmfff…"

My body bucked and shook as Dennis stroked every drop of cum from my dick. When he was done he walked me to the door of the room, opened it, and pushed me out, right into the waiting hands of two of the guys at the party. Actually, they were two of the guys from the opposing baseball college team that we had creamed today.

"Hey Hot shot, great fucking game today huh?" one of the guys asked me as he held me by my arm, running his other hand over my chest. "That was a great homer you hit, won your team the game. Never thought that I would get to hit my own homerun with you though. Fuck man, we got the star player of the opposing team here."

"He sure is hot shit huh Simon?" the other guy asked as he squeezed my butt cheeks a few times. "I was checking him out like crazy during the game. Smells like a damned locker room though."

"That's okay Roger," Simon said to his friend and stole a sniff at one of my armpits. "It turns me on more."

Dennis vacated the room he had just worked me over in. Holding me by my arms Simon and Roger brought me back into that room.

"Mmmmmfff…" I wailed miserably.

They stood me against a wall with my back to them, pulled my baseball uniform pants down in the back, and knelt behind me. They each kissed, licked, and bit one of my butt cheeks hard.

"Fuck his tits," Simon said breathlessly. "These hot bubble butt buns of his are where it's at."

"I'll second that," Roger said and clamped his teeth down on one of my butt cheeks.

"RRRRmmmmffff…" I sputtered angrily as the two guys feasted on my butt cheeks.

I felt them biting down hard on my cheeks and running their hands over them, licking them, kissing them. I was sweating profusely from anger, fear, and humiliation all at once. Damn Rocky and Mark for getting me into this and damn myself for daring those two bastards to suck my nipples. I should have known that they would find some way to get back at me for that. But not this not a bunch of perverts feasting on me as if I was some cheap whore. I writhed against the wall as Roger and Simon now licked my butt cheeks hard, soaking them with their saliva. Once again my dick was hard in my pants. Could it be that somewhere deep inside myself *I was* actually enjoying all this shit??? Roger and Simon finally stopped working on my butt cheeks and brought me out of the room and to the main room where the party was in full swing. A few minutes later I found myself sitting on a couch between two guys who were having a grand old time squeezing and twisting my sore nipples while they sipped beers. Another guy was squatting in front of me, stroking my dick, which was still in my pants. The two guys sitting on my sides spilled beer onto my nipples and sucked it off hard, over and over and over again. I was sweating miserably and in a state of forced ecstasy. I looked across the room at Rocky and Mark with fire in my eyes. Then the guy stroking my dick through my pants stopped. Then, a guy that everybody was calling Chip helped me up off the couch. Chip walked me out of the main party room and down a flight of stairs to a basement. What was I in for now I wondered miserably? Chip told me he had a strong fetish for baseball players, especially baseball players who hit homeruns, adding that he liked to suck their bats. I stood there helplessly as Chip pulled my hard dick out of the fly opening of my pants, kneeled down in front of me, and slurped my boner into his mouth. As he sucked me he ran his big paw-like hands up and down my legs, gently caressing them. I had never had a guy suck my dick before, but then I had never been in a position like this before. I found I was actually enjoying what Chip was doing to me. His big hands moved all over my legs as he sucked me harder and harder. He grabbed my butt cheeks and pulled me closer to himself, pulling my dick into his throat. Then, I shot my third load. Chip swallowed it all, smacking his lips together as my dick slipped out of his mouth. I was shaking in ecstasy, trembling, and gasping.

"Mmmmmffffff!!!" I moaned loudly as Chip stood up, leaving my dick sticking out of my pants.

"Got something you want to say Cliff?" Chip asked me.

I nodded that I did as sweat dripped down off my forehead. Chip said that he would take the sock out of my mouth, but just so I could say what I had to say, then I would be gagged again. I nodded that I understood. He took the foul tasting sock out of my mouth and I licked my lips before speaking.

"Th-thanks Chip," I said as he ran a hand through my champagne soaked hair. "Listen man, I haven't had time to take a piss since the game earlier today. I have to fucking piss like you would not believe. Could I please use the bathroom down here before you bring me back upstairs?"

He looked at me and smiled. Then, he crammed the sock back into my mouth and tied the other one over it. Still smiling, he again squatted down in front of me.

"Always wanted to drink a hot baseball player's piss," Chip said and slurped the tip of my dick between his lips.

"Hrrrrrmmmfff..." I squealed, looking down at him in total disbelief.

He suckled the tip of my dick, poked his tongue tip into it, and I found myself pissing into the guy's mouth. He gulped down my sour tasting hot piss, a look of sheer ecstasy on his face.

"RRRRmmmfff..." I gasped as I pissed and pissed.

When I was done Chip packed my dick back into my pants and brought me back upstairs to the party. Guys passed me around, squeezed my nipples hard, smacked me hard on the ass, and squeezed my crotch. It was more than three hours later when Rocky and Mark carried me out to their van and drove me back to the locker room at the college. I was exhausted, spent, and mortified all at once. They stood over me as I sat on the bench in front of my locker. They untied my hands and took the sock gag out of my mouth. I sat there massaging my numb wrists, looking up at them.

"I hope you're not angry at us Cliff," Rocky said. "You made us suck your smelly tits after all."

I looked at my nipples and saw that it would be days before they looked normal again. I squeezed one of them and grimaced.

"And the party wasn't all that bad," Mark said. "It just shows you that a bunch of guys can have a lot of fun when they really want to."

I looked at both of them blankly.

"Come on Cliff, say something man," Rocky said. "Please don't say you're not our friend anymore."

Finally, I smiled.

"Not be your friend?" I asked them. "Guys, *when the fuck is the next party?*"

We all laughed and Rocky and Mark happily hoisted me to their shoulders. They carried me to the showers where we all had more fun. This time though I wasn't tied up and gagged…

Rubber Pig

Written by: Anonymous Cop and added onto by Christopher Trevor

It was Rubber night at the sleazy club called "The Local", but after a few hours of chatting with friends and having a couple of submissives tongue clean my boots and buy me some beers I decided to leave and head on home. I was just not in the mood that night, even though being dressed in neck-to-toe tight black latex always turned me hard, my mind was just not with it. Driving back to my secluded house beyond the city limits I tried to figure out what was itching at me, making me discontent. Maybe it was the sameness of my life and perhaps I needed a new challenge; maybe a trip to London or Amsterdam where the rubber life was far more active. Don't get me wrong, I have a great life here; a substantial inheritance from my parents, coupled with my own astute investments left me well off and capable of buying whatever I wanted. I had the house, this brand new Mercedes, all the rubber/leather gear any man with my fetishes would want, a homemade dungeon to indulge my fetishes in, and basically an adequate sex life. Well, that is to say that there were always submissive men and fags around willing to drop to their knees or lean over to suck and fuck and do whatever the hell I wanted. But something was missing and I wasn't sure of exactly just what it was.

I should have been paying more attention to my driving because after I pulled onto the side of the road off the main highway that led to my place I caught the blue flashing lights of one of the counties sheriff department cruisers. Damn, I thought, not again. It seems like every time I was on the road at night I got stopped by one of those bastards. Well, there was nothing to do but pull over and let the pig lecture and ticket me. Man, this was getting boring; it was the fourth or fifth time in the last couple of months.

I pulled to the side of the road and the cruiser pulled in behind me. Having learned from a cop buddy a long time ago I turned on the car's interior lights and put both of my hands on top of the steering wheel. This, my friend said lets the cop see me, lets him know I that I'm not an immediate threat and that I'm not trying anything dumb. I watched as the cop exited his vehicle and approached mine. He was about five foot ten, give or take, in his mid thirties, seemingly in good shape, hatless, showing his marine style haircut. He walked with purpose and I noticed that his low quarter shoes were gleaming from the spit shine he must have given them. He was wearing what I assumed was the regulation county uniform- dark blue trousers, a light blue shirt and tie, a belt full of cop gear on his waist and a black leather jacket. As he got closer I recognized him as one of the cops who had pulled me over a couple of times before and ticketed me. I lowered the window and looked up at him.

From the look on his face I could see that he was taken aback by my outfit and I realized that it must indeed have looked strange to see someone in tight black rubber. But he was professional and he recovered quickly by asking for my license and registration, which I handed over. The cop took them and went back to his cruiser, most likely to check his computer and verify that I wasn't some wanted or escaped convict or serial killer. When he returned he asked me, and very politely I might add, always referring to me as "Sir" to please get out of the car, put my hands on the trunk and spread my legs. I knew there wasn't much point in arguing so I did as ordered with just a shrug. He asked if I had any weapons or needles on me or anything that might stick him. I half laughed and said, "Officer, I think you can see from how my outfit clings to me that there isn't any place I could hide anything."

"I just want to make sure Sir." he responded politely.

Then, he proceeded to pat me down, although damned if I knew what the hell he was looking for. His leather gloved hands quickly rubbed down my arms, chest, stomach and legs. Maybe it was just my overactive imagination but I could have sworn that he spent a tad longer than necessary at my crotch area, almost tenderly caressing the areas of my cock and balls. They were encased in a thicker rubber cod-piece which snapped onto the sides of the tight latex pants I was wearing. Actually, the cop's hands felt kind of nice there and for one wild moment I thought I might get aroused, but he took his hands away and the moment was gone.

I heard the radio in his cruiser make some loud static-like noise and he said, "You can relax now Sir. Just let me check my vehicle again and I'll be back."

He was gone for a few minutes and when he returned he handed me back my papers and apologized.

"Sorry about this Sir," he said. "We've had a report of a stolen Mercedes and I had to make sure this wasn't it. You're free to go now Sir. Have a nice night."

I got back in my car and drove off wondering what in hell that was really all about. But at least I didn't get another ticket so I suppose I should have been grateful. Some day I would make those damned deputies pay for all the tickets they handed out. But still, that cop's attitude didn't make much sense, no sense at all. It was almost as if he just wanted to feel me up, crazy!

When I got home I had a beer and some snacks and sat down to watch a rubber bondage DVD which had arrived earlier in the week. I hadn't had time to view it so I figured it was appropriate to keep my rubber on while watching. I did undo the cod-piece though and let my eight plus inches fall loose. It was a long film, over two hours, unusual for porn, but worth it. It had a meaningless plot and it starred two well-built guys captured by an equally well-built sadist who put them in head to toe rubber and a lot of different bondage positions, ah, fun times had by all.

It was after one AM so I was surprised when I heard the doorbell ring. I looked out the window and saw a Dodge Ram van parked in my driveway, but not recognizing it I checked the video camera over my door. I was totally surprised to see the pig cop who had stopped me earlier.

"Oh shit," I said to myself. "Now what???"

I buttoned up my cod-piece before I opened the door.

The cop stood there, looking a bit hesitant and unsure, but I noticed that he eyed me up and down before he spoke.

"Sir, I'm sorry to bother you at this hour, but I saw your light on so I hoped you were still awake," the cop said.

"Yes Officer, no problem. "What can I do for you?"

"Well Sir," (and I admit I enjoyed his calling me Sir), "I didn't notice it until after I signed off duty but I forgot to return your driver's license when I stopped you earlier tonight," the cop said. "Apparently I gave you back your registration but forgot about the license. I got your address from it and thought I would get it to you as soon as I could. Here it is, and I am sorry Sir."

He handed me the license. I hadn't even checked when he had handed me back my papers. I had just shoved them into my wallet. But something was wrong about all this. Cops don't forget to hand back licenses. I had a thought and decided to follow it through.

"Well thanks Officer...?" I began.

"Langston," he answered. "Craig Langston."

"Well Officer Langston...Craig...this is really considerate of you to bring my license here in person," I said. "You could have mailed it to me. I really do appreciate it. You said you were off duty now. Why don't you come in and have a beer, if that's okay."

"Yes Sir, I'm off duty for the next couple of days," the cop replied. "I really shouldn't drink while in uniform but damn it's been a rough night and I'd love a beer."

I couldn't believe it. In a short time the pig cop was sitting in my living room, drinking a beer and chatting. We talked about a couple of mundane things, the weather, the local sports teams, what it's like being a cop etc. I asked him why it was that I was stopped so often and ticketed. He looked sort of embarrassed and stammered slightly but finally replied.

"Well, you see, that sector is kind of lonely, not much happening and just to break the monotony we tend to stop anyone even who's even slightly over the speed limit, anything just for something to do in the late hours."

I decided to test him a little further.

"Were you influenced because you thought I was gay?" I asked.

He frowned deeper and then sort of grinned, and I must admit that when he smiled he was a handsome looking man. His deep blue eyes seemed to sparkle and his lips looked excitingly tempting when parted in a laugh.

"Well, to be honest, some of the guys actually did enjoy harassing you because you are…" he said but then hesitated some more. "… well, queer I suppose is the word used nowadays. Those guys get a laugh or two back at the squad room telling about stopping you and other, uh, queers."

"And how about you?" I asked. "Do you get a laugh from ticketing a gay man?"

"Oh no, no, honest, I don't care one way or the other what you do in the privacy of your own home," the cop said. "I'm not anti-gay or anything, honest. I suppose I stopped you because I was just lonely out there on the road and it was nice to have someone to talk to, even if just to give a ticket."

The cop was clearly embarrassed by the conversation so I thought it best to change the subject. I offered him another beer which he quickly accepted. All the time he was talking he was obviously trying very hard not to look at my rubber outfit, but failing. Finally, he said, "Excuse me Sir, but is that rubber you have on?"

And then I knew I had him.

"Yes," I said. "It's a fetish of mine. I love the feel of the warm latex rubber on my body. It just makes me feel great. Have you ever worn any rubber Craig?"

I was speaking confidently and used his first name because I wanted him to think we were becoming friends.

"No," he replied. "I have some boots and waders that I use when I go fishing and of course my rubber rain gear as part of my uniform. I like the feel of them, but I've never had anything like what you're wearing now. It looks so…well, interesting. Doesn't it make you sweat or something…?"

He wasn't sure what it was he wanted to ask.

"Oh yeah, a little, but just enough to feel good," I replied. "It's hard to put into words but its like the latex forms another layer of skin over my own. It's a warm, rubbery feeling. Rubbery, not sure that that's a real word but I can't think of any other description that says it better. It's all so damned comforting. If I were one of those psych doctors, like that TV guy Doctor Phil, I'd probably say its like still being in the womb- corny, but actually true."

I noticed my cop friend's right hand was slightly shaking and I interpreted the look in his eyes as pure need; the bastard wanted the rubber. I walked over to him and stood there.

"Feel it yourself," I said almost commandingly. "This time feel it without your gloves on like you did on the road. Feel how smooth it is. As I said, it's like a second skin. It feels better when you're wearing it."

And he couldn't resist. His hand reached out and soon he was rubbing…well, maybe caressing is a better word…the upper part of my leg and then my chest. Man, he was practically drooling at this point.

"You know," I said. "You and I are about the same size. I have lots of rubber gear and if you'd like to try some on it's no problem. Just to get the feel of it. I think you might enjoy that. What do you say?"

The pig didn't even hesitate.

"Hell yeah, I would like that," he said. "I mean, if it isn't too much bother."

"No bother at all," I replied. "I think I have just the gear for you. How big are you by the way?"

"I'm five foot ten and I weigh in at one hundred and seventy five pounds Sir," he responded.

"Perfect Officer, you'll fit easily into my gear," I said. "Come on into the other room and we'll see what we can do."

We went into what I call my dressing room, the space where I keep all my leather and rubber gear. I could see his eyes taking in all the gear hanging from racks, the dozens of boots and jackets, gloves, along with pants and shirts, in both leather and rubber.

"Wow," he said. "You sure have a big collection of stuff."

"Well, as I said, it is a fetish with me," I reiterated. "And I can afford it so why not. Now the first thing you have to do is get out of that uniform. No way can you wear rubber over it."

I had said it jokingly about him taking off his uniform but I could tell that he was a tad hesitant about that. I'm sure that the thought of having to strip out of his uniform had obviously not entered his mind. I tried to make it a little easier on him by pointing out a leather bench nearby with some hooks and clothes hangers near it.

"You can hang your clothes there, so they don't get wrinkled," I said, as if I really gave a shit whether or not his uniform got wrinkled. "While you change I'll see what I can come up with that will fit you, although we're both roughly the same size so it shouldn't be hard."

I turned my back on him and went to the other side of the room, ostensibly looking for the right gear, but actually I knew exactly what I wanted him in. I dawdled for a few minutes to give him time, picked out a black latex cat suit that fit tightly on the body and had a cod-piece at the crotch. It also had small patches at each nip which could be unsnapped for access to those areas and a zipper at the ass for easy access there as well. When I turned and headed back to the cop I saw that he was naked from the waist up and was sitting on the bench, working at removing his shoes. I noted again the sparkling spit shine on his shoes and thought what a fine job he'd do on my leather boots. He removed the shoes and then hesitantly dropped his uniform pants and slid them off. He was obviously a little nervous about this but I read the determination on his face that now that he had committed himself to this he was going to follow through all the way. He placed the uniform pants on a hanger and hung them on a hook. Then, he sat down to remove his nearly knee high silk black socks which clung tightly to his shapely feet and strong ankles. I admit I'm a foot man; love guys with great looking feet…and his were most impressive. He slid his socks off and then stood, naked except for a pair of tight white jockey shorts. I could see from the bulge in those shorts that this cop had a more than respectable basket and I could also see that despite his not wanting to, his cock was getting hard. Once again I thought to myself, "You are mine pig, you are mine."

I reached for a big towel and tossed it to him.

"Getting into rubber isn't always easy to do," I explained. "It doesn't slide on quickly and if you're hairy or sweaty it's even harder. I can see that you're nicely smooth so that isn't a problem, but use the towel to dry yourself off as best you can."

He took the towel and although I was pretending not to, I watched out of the corner of my eye and he did indeed present a fine figure as he rubbed his well developed chest, nice abs and even his armpits. He did his legs, raising one and then the other in turn and finally realized that he had to remove his briefs and do his crotch. I was right; that was one beautiful dick belonging to that cop; over nine inches long I'm sure when it was hard and thick too. But best of all were his balls…nice large low hangers; perfect for some well planned ball torture. When he was finished he stood there in a sort of parade rest stance and this time it was me who was taken aback. Yes, this was one fine looking dude.

"Okay," I said. "First thing you have to do is powder your body. A little of this talc and the rubber slides on more easily.

I handed him a container of talc and while he powdered his body I applied a thin layer to the inside of the cat suit.

"Normally a person would use a latex cock sheath for his cock and balls but since you're just trying the gear on this time, we can skip that," I said. "Here, this is cat suit. Note that it is zippered up in the back, so what you have to do is step into it feet first and get it on up to your waist. Take it slow but once you have it on work with your hands to smooth the rubber out and bring it up to your waist so that it clings to your body. It may be a little awkward until you get used to it, but it'll help you."

As I instructed him he sat on the bench and eased first one leg and then the other into the cat suit, working his toes into the foot part of the outfit. It was a joy to watch this hunk cop wiggle and squirm, pulling the black latex up over his muscular legs. It took him over ten minutes before he had the suit on up to his waist.

"Now," I said. "You have to smooth it out. What you do is work your hands up the rubber, smoothing out any air bumps or snags. Work it as a kind of ripple effect. It's best to start with your feet. Here, let me show you what I mean."

Damn I had wanted to get at those feet ever since I spotted them in the knee high thin black socks. Now was my chance. I knelt in front of the cop, paying no attention to his semi-erect cock bulging against the rubber. I took his left foot in my hands and began to gently ease the rubber forward, up the ankle to the calf. Then the right foot. The sensation of fondling those rubber encased feet sent a bolt of excitement and desire through me and I could feel my own cock getting hard inside the rubber cod-piece. I figured I'd better not push my luck and stopped below the knees.

"Okay Craig, I think you get the idea now," I said. "Work the rest of it up to your waist and then we'll finish putting the suit on you."

It was interesting to me that the cop hadn't said a word since we started. He was far too into the rubber to think straight, never mind talk. He smiled at me a couple of times when he obviously felt the smoothness of the latex against his skin, but still said nothing.

"Okay," I said. "Now comes the top. This is much easier. What you have to do is work your arms into the sleeves and pull the suit up and over your chest and back. Once you get that done I'll zip up the back and we'll see how it feels."

Again it was exciting to watch as he worked the top of the cat suit over his chest, easing his arms into the sleeves and pulling it tight. He looked magnificent, I have to admit, his was a body made to be encased in rubber.

"Great," I said when he had finished. "Now just let me zip up the back and we're almost done."

I carefully pulled the zipper up from his waist to his neck. It was a little tight because he was just a bit bigger in the chest area than I am but I did it.

"Now let's see what you look like so far," I said, taking in the sight of him. "Yes, looking good. Now flex your knees and twirl your arms and walk around to have the rubber settle into your body."

I watched as he took some knee bends, twisted and pumped his arms and bent over to touch his toes. I had to hold myself back from taking him right then and there.

"How does it feel?" I asked.

"Fantastic," he replied. "Like you said, it's almost like a second skin, a part of me. I've never had a sensation that felt quite like this."

I pulled aside a curtain to reveal a full-length mirror.

"Here, look at yourself," I said. "What do you think now?"

"Fuck," was the first word out of his mouth. "Followed by, "Goddamn, this is something!"

"Ah yes, my new friend," I said. "But we're not done yet. What size boot do you wear?"

"Eleven and a half wide," he answered.

"Well, I'm only a ten so I don't think any of my regular calf-length rubber boots will fit you," I said. "So I suppose this time you'll have to make do with some hip boots. Let me get you a pair."

I secretly watched him flexing and gawking into the mirror while I went for the boots. He didn't seem embarrassed or self conscious, but then again I don't think he really noticed that I was in the room with him. He was too immersed in how he looked in the rubber gear.

"Here we go," I said, handing him a pair of hip-high rubber boots. "Just pull these on over the cat suit. While you do that I'll get some gloves and a hood."

The boots were a tad too small for his feet but that made it all the better because they seemed to cling to those muscular legs of his. He kept them folded down at the knees at first, and I think that was because he so enjoyed looking at the tight latex clinging to his legs.

"Okay, now we're ready for a hood," I said. "Or to be more precise, you're ready for a hood. No rubber outfit is complete without a hood. I wear one around here a lot, but I took it off when you rang my bell. Now this is a good one. It has eye and nose holes big enough to see and breathe through and the mouth hole is large enough so as not to interfere with eating."

Of course I didn't tell him just what it would be that he would be eating, but I figured he'd find out soon enough. I fitted the hood over his head, pulling it slowly down so the face-holes matched up in the proper places. It fit snugly and the small zipper on the back tightened it even more. It had a full length neck which reached down beyond the upper limits of the cat suit so I pulled down the suit's zipper just enough to insert the rubber neck from the hood and then zipped it back up. I then got out a one and a half inch rubber collar and placed it on his neck, strapping it tightly but not so much as to strangle him or to interfere with his breathing. He didn't seem to notice and didn't offer any resistance, even when I padlocked the collar in the rear, making it impossible to remove without the key.

"Look at yourself now," I said. "Recognize yourself at all?"

He looked in the mirror again and I could tell it was like he was hypnotized. He could not stop staring.

"Final pieces of gear are these tight latex gloves," I said. "Here, put them on. Don't worry; they'll stretch to fit your hands."

I wish I could better describe what an absolutely beautiful rubber picture this pig cop presented. A man made to be in rubber, that's what he was. Better yet a man made to be in rubber and kneeling at my feet. Getting him into that position created a minor problem, but I figured that this cop was so into the rubber he was ready to obey any suggestion I made.

I spoke softly and smoothly to him, not wanting to break him from the obvious rubber spell he was in.

"You know boy, some people were born to be in rubber," I said soothingly. "They come alive when encased in the warm sensuous embrace of pure rubber and latex. I think you're one of those people, boy. What do you think?"

He hadn't stopped rubbing his chest and stomach, feeling the rubber clinging to his body. At first I didn't think the pig had heard me, but then he replied, "Yes, you're right. I feel so alive and warm and secure. It's wonderful…a feeling I've never had or known before."

He was looking at me but I'm not sure he was actually seeing me. I moved up next to him and started to run my hands up and down his slick rubber covered body. I rubbed his legs and lingered on the cheeks of his muscular ass. He seemed to cringe as I handled his ass cheeks through the rubber but he eventually calmed again. While gently squeezing his ass, I pulled him close to me, leaned into his chest and began licking the rubber. I could feel him tense up again as my tongue slithered and kissed the area of his nips, all the while my hands played gently with that sexy ass of his. He moaned and I could sense his cock getting harder inside the rubber so I reached down and even more gently began fondling it. I could tell this was a huge turn-on for the handsome deputy as his breathing came faster and harder, so I stopped. I didn't want him satisfying himself until he had satisfied me.

I whispered to him, "Boy, as good as the rubber feels and looks, it tastes even better. Lick my chest and my nips boy, you'll see what I mean." I gently maneuvered his face against my own rubber covered chest and it took no more urging than that before the cop was furiously licking away. Oh God, did that feel good! I was getting so turned on that I could not believe it. Slowly, carefully I pushed the cop's head down and in back so he was licking my ass. While I was doing this I unsnapped the cod-piece that covered my crotch and let my now almost totally hard cock flop out. I maneuvered the cop's head around as he continued to lick the rubber and suddenly he was directly facing my cock.

"Lick it boy," I said.

He stared at my cock, his mouth open, his tongue flickering. What a sight that was let me tell you. He then looked up at my face but quickly stared back at my cock.

"No," he said. "I can't...I don't...I'm not queer...I don't..." he stammered.

Actual words seemed to fail him but he never took his eyes off my swelling member.

Quietly, evenly, gently I said, "It's okay boy. Don't worry. But I know you do want this boy. You want to know what a man's cock tastes like. You always have. I can see it in your eyes. Now is your chance, while in your rubber. You want to do it boy and it's good. It's all right."

"No, no, please Sir, don't make me do it..." he pleaded.

"Make you?" I asked him. "Make you do what boy?"

"Suck your cock Sir," he responded. "I...I never... Don't make me do it."

"I'm not making you do it boy, you want to do it," I said calmly. "You want to taste your Master's cock, the cock of a real rubber man. Do it because you want to do it boy."

He continued staring at my cock as if it were a cobra type of snake hypnotizing him.

"Please Sir..." he whispered.

"It's okay boy, I know, I understand," I said soothingly and caressed the top of his rubber covered head. "Just lick the head of my cock there. Then just gently kiss it and then lick it, that's all."

He hesitated for a second or two and then his tongue reached out even further and he licked the tip of my cock. It jumped a little at his gentle touch and he pulled back, but damn if he didn't get right back on it. And he was licking that cock head, all around it, oh man!

"Good boy," I said as I gently rubbed his head. "Now, lick the shaft, just lick up and down."

And soon he was licking up and down and up and down the now hard and throbbing shaft of my manhood. He stopped only to lick and suck on one of my balls and then the other. It didn't take much persuasion on my part before he had a good part of the cock in his mouth. He immediately gagged on it but amazingly adjusted his throat muscles and got right back on it. Although I suspected that Deputy Craig Langston had never previously sucked a man's cock, it was obvious that he was a natural at it. Soon the two of us were in perfect synch as he sucked in unison with my thrusts and moves. I held the back of his rubber covered head and kept him from backing off when I knew that I could not hold off any longer…and spurt after spurt of warm cum erupted into his throat. And again I was amazed that he didn't try to pull back but instead swallowed and gulped it all down…and kept on sucking even when there was no more left in me.

I pulled out of his mouth and looked down at him.

"Look at me boy," I ordered.

He looked up and I was surprised to see that despite the rubber hood covering his face, the traces of a smile had turned the corners of his mouth. Not only was this man made to be in rubber, he was made to serve other men, and I was just the dominant to teach him the ways to do that.

"Well boy, do you know what this means?" I asked him. "You just sucked off another man and swallowed his manly juice. Only fags and slaves do that. We know you aren't a fag; after all you are a county deputy, so you must be a slave. Or at least a slave in the making isn't that true boy?"

He was very obviously puzzled and still a bit bedazzled by what had happened to him. I could tell he was having trouble trying to understand what I had just said to him.

"But I'm a cop," was all that came out of him.

"Cops can be slaves too you know boy," I replied. "It's your inner nature that dictates your position in life. You chose to be a cop and that is great for your outer nature. It's a noble, worthwhile job and one that you should be proud of. You protect and serve the community. But your inner nature is screaming out to serve a man in a different way too. You want to serve a man who can dominate and control you and satisfy that urge you have. That is the slave in you boy."

"But how?" he asked. "I mean, I don't know what to do. I've never done this before. And if the other guys in the department find out I'll be laughed off the force. I'm confused Sir."

"Yes boy, I know," I said. "Don't worry. I'll train you and it will be our secret. No one will find out; none of the other cops will ever know. When you are on duty you will be the best damned deputy on the force, but off duty you will belong to me boy. Do you understand?"

"I'm not sure Sir, I think so, but all this happened so fast," he replied. "I mean…when I came here I was wearing my uniform…now I'm dressed in rubber…I mean, shit, I don't know what I mean Sir."

"Admit it boy, you deliberately held back my driver's license because you wanted an excuse to come here and see for yourself," I responded. "You stopped me those other times because you just couldn't resist. You want this boy, *you want to serve me*. And you shall. Now crawl over here and clean my boots with your tongue."

This was the test; this was the moment which would decide the cop's fate. He could say no, get up, and remove the rubber, get dressed and leave…and that would be that. Or he could do as ordered.

He hesitated only a second then crawled to my feet and began licking the boots.

"Good slave," I said. "You have a lot to learn to be the slave that will make you proud of yourself as well as your Master," I said. "But I can train you, no fear my boy. It won't be easy on you; it will be punishing and debasing and at times torturous, but you will see it through and in the end you'll be a changed man, I promise. When you do as you should you can wear the rubber you so obviously get pleasure from. But when you disobey or don't obey fast enough or displease me in any way, then it won't be pleasure you receive."

"Yes Sir," my new rubber slave murmured as he continued licking my rubber boots clean.

"The first rule slave is that you will call me MASTER at all times," I instructed. "Anyone else you meet will be addressed as "SIR", but I am always "MASTER." "Do you understand?"

"Yes Master," he replied.

"The second thing is that you will never speak unless spoken to and then your responses will be to the point, either "Yes Master, No Master or Thank you Master." "Understand slave?" I asked him.

"Yes Master," he replied again.

"Good slave boy," I said. "Now, I want to show you my main room where you'll be spending a lot of your time.

While he knelt there I took a dog leash from the wall and attached it to his collar. I tugged on it and led him toward the rear door which was the entrance to my dungeon. As we passed the mirror I stopped.

"Look at yourself slave boy," I ordered. "You are like a dog now. Bark like a dog."

The cop looked into the mirror and I swear that if he had a tail he would have been wagging it furiously by then.

"Woof, woof," he barked.

I laughed and led him through the door to the dungeon. I could tell he was shocked at what he saw- the rack, the chains, the cuffs attached to the wall, the cages, the whips and other torture devices. He hesitated a little but I jerked on the leash and he continued to follow me like a good rubber puppy dog.

"This is my dungeon slave boy, a room where I'll be training you to be the slave you so desperately want to be," I explained as he looked around. "You'll grow to love and hate this room but it will be the beginning of your new life. Now, it's late and we've both had long days so I think it's time for some sleep. You said you have a few days off so I won't worry about you missing work boy. Hmmm, I definitely have to come up with a new name for you; can't keep calling you just boy or slave boy. Oh well, I'll think of one later. Right now I want you to climb up on this table, it's a reconstructed version of a doctor's operating table, but don't worry I'm not going to operate on you."

This was obviously a man who couldn't wait to redo his life as he was up on the table in a flash. The table was built with rounded hooks at the end and I spread his legs and tied one ankle to each hook. Then I fastened his arms and wrists to the sides of the table and he was totally secure for the night. I left him for a minute while I went back to my wardrobe room for one more piece of rubber gear. It was another hood but this one was different in that instead of a mouth hole it had a small but effective rubber gag which fit nicely into the deputy's mouth, thus making speech difficult, but not interfering with his breathing. There was no eye holes in this hood so all light and sight were cut off. It had a few small holes at the nose which allowed breathing and I knew from experimenting on myself that it was more than sufficient. I took the hood off him that he was wearing and pulled the new one over the cop's head, tightening it down with straps, then used other straps to affix his head tightly to the table. In effect he could not move at all now.

"Comfy my little asshole slave boy?" I asked.

The muffled moan which came through the hood I took as a "Yes Master", but I could have been wrong, har, har, har.

I turned on the video/audio monitors so I could watch my new slave from the comfort of my bedroom and as I was walking out I noted that the bulge in his rubber covered crotch was throbbing. I figured the dumb cop had gone through a lot for his first night as a slave and deserved some sort of reward. I unsnapped the cod-piece from his crotch and pulled his now hard and pulsating cock out into the air. I put on a pair of tight latex gloves and slowly but firmly began to stroke that beautiful cock. I could hear the moans and groans and sighs coming from the hooded pig as I played with his cock. I could almost guess that he was begging me to let him cum. Normally I wouldn't have allowed that, but since I wanted him to be a one hundred percent rubber slave I succumbed and working just a bit faster and smoother brought him to the edge. Then I stopped. I heard his moans and, I'm sure, pleadings from within the hood but I just laughed.

"Ah my horny little rubber slave, you want release do you?" I asked him. "I want to hear you tell me what a good slave boy you're going to be. When I hear that then maybe I'll let you cum. What do you say boy?"

Of course I couldn't understand any of the sounds and groans and moans that came forth from the tied down cop, but I knew he was screaming that he would be the best slave I ever had. And I believed him.

It didn't take much the second time of stroking to bring him to release. The amount of cop cum that poured forth from that beautiful cock of his really was something to see as it splattered and splashed over the black latex on his stomach. I left it there, knowing that in the morning he would have to clean that rubber with his tongue. I patted him on his rubber covered face and said, "Good night my pet, tomorrow your new life begins."

In my bedroom I turned on my monitor and watched as this rubbered hunk stirred slightly in his bondage. Damned but the pig was hard again. That's when I decided his new name would be Porky, no; I quickly changed my mind, not Porky, but Petunia. That would really bring him down. Petunia Pig…ha, ha, that was great, that was fucking great. I knew now that I had a mission, something to keep me happy and occupied for the coming months. My goal would be to train this cop into being a total pig slave, reacting immediately to any and all orders. I would approach it like the Marine Corps, breaking him down completely and then rebuilding him the way I wanted him to be. It was a task I was looking forward to. And knowing myself I knew that once I had succeeded I would grow tired of him and sell him off. Or perhaps I would give him away to some other MASTER who would debase and degrade him even more. That would teach the fucker for giving me those tickets.

The Marine and the Scoundrels

Scoundrels…bastards…low life's… Those are the only words I can find to describe what those two guys are. What they did to me… what they allowed to have done to me…no one, *no one,* especially a United States marine should have to suffer such degradation and humiliation. Let me calm down here and tell you my story. I want to tell it just to make sure it doesn't ever happen again to another marine. My name is Clifton Davis, I'm twenty two years old, I'm from Georgia, and I'm proud to be able to say I'm a United States marine. I have blond hair, (cut really short-military style, high and tight as it's called in the service) blue eyes, a round face, and a very toned and muscular body from basic training. After boot camp I was lucky enough to be stationed in my hometown of Georgia. Still, I had hoped to be stationed in New York City. After my first year anniversary in the marines my commanding officer granted me a week's leave. Needless to say I decided to spend it in the big apple. With the money I had saved I flew to New York on a non-stop flight from Georgia and checked in at a semi-luxurious hotel on the Upper East Side. Once I was settled in I decided to go out and do some sight seeing. Dressed in my olive colored uniform and a camera around my neck I left the hotel. I saw the statue of liberty, the world trade center, (this story was written before 9/11) and rode the train just for fun. Around two in the afternoon I found I was feeling pretty hungry so I decided to have a late lunch. I returned to my hotel and stopped at the bar in the lobby to have a couple of drinks before lunch...just to sort of whet my appetite before lunch. I sat up on a bar stool and ordered a scotch and water. The bartender served me quickly and called me Sir as he put the glass down in front of me.

"To the United States..." I said proudly and raised my glass to the bartender.

He smiled as I took a sip of my drink and went over to serve the two guys at the other end of the bar who had been sitting there when I came in. When I was halfway through my drink the bartender set a second one down in front of me.

"I didn't order a second drink Sir." I said to him politely.

"It's from the two guys at the end of the bar." the bartender said to me. "They asked if you would accept a drink from them as their respect for the military."

I looked down at the end of the bar and the two guys (both of them pretty big and burly looking-sort of construction worker types I guess...) raised their beer cans to me. I smiled, raised my half done glass of scotch and water, and gulped it down. The bartender took my empty glass away as I took the one that had been bought for me in hand. I took a sip of it and realized it was straight scotch.

"Hooo whee..." I said with a grin. "Now that is a drink fit for a fucking marine..."

Not to be impolite I stood up, put my hat under my arm, picked up my drink, and walked over to the two men.

"Thank you for the scotch you guys." I said and placed the glass down on the bar.

I held out my hand and they each shook it.

"I'm Clifton Davis, U.S. marine." I said proudly.

"Nice to meet you Sir." the first guy said to me politely. "I'm Cleeve and this here is my buddy Otis."

"Good to meet you." Otis said to me. "So, where are you stationed?"

"My hometown, Georgia." I replied, my Southern accent setting in real thick and sexy and took a sip of my scotch. "I'm here in New York on a sort of celebration...I've been a marine for a year now..."

"Ah, now that calls for another drink..." Cleeve said, signaling the bartender.

"No, no really, thank you...but I'm going to have a late lunch pretty soon." I said to Cleeve.

"Nothing is too good for our boys in the service." Cleeve said. "Especially one as handsome as you Clifton."

"Well thank you Sir." I said in a very southern sounding accent now. "I guess it would be downright impolite of me to refuse another drink then."

"Sure would be..." Otis said and squeezed my arm.

As I sipped my second drink the bartender set a third glass of scotch on the bar in front of Cleeve and Otis.

"So, are you staying here at the hotel?" Cleeve asked me.

"Sure am." I said and sipped my drink again. "Saved enough money so I would be able to stay in a real nice hotel and really enjoy your city."

"Been sight seeing?" Otis asked me.

"Sure have been." I replied.

As I sipped my second drink I told the two men (who both seemed so polite and friendly) of the sights I had seen so far on my first day in New York. When I was finished with my second drink I placed the empty glass on the bar and Otis quickly handed me the third drink. Not to be impolite I took it from him and sipped it.

"That's it Sir, drink up..." Otis said.

Being that I had not yet eaten I was already feeling pretty dizzy and somewhat disoriented from the first two drinks I had consumed. The third one would have me flying for sure but as I sipped it I promised myself that I would eat right after I was done with it...*right.* When I was halfway through my third drink I noticed that I was slurring a little as I continued speaking with Cleeve and Otis.

"So how long are you in New York for?" Cleeve asked me.

"A we-week..." I replied, feeling drunk at that point. "I think that's enough scotch for now..."

As I went to put my half full glass on the bar Cleeve gently grabbed me by wrist.

"Now, now, it would be downright improper for you not to finish that drink Sir." Cleeve said to me.

"I'm uh, not really feeling all that well at the moment..." I managed to say.

"Finish your drink and we'll help you up to your room." Otis suggested as Cleeve guided my hand with the glass in it toward my mouth. "What room are you in anyway?"

"Fourteen zero six." I replied and sipped the scotch.

"That's it boy, drink up..." Cleeve said with a grin on his face. "Fuckin' marines can down scotch like it's water..."

"Not this one..." I thought miserably.

When I was done with the third drink I had to lean on the bar to keep myself balanced.

"Man oh fuckin' man..." I said, trying to sound macho. "The fucking room is spinning..."

"C'mon Otis, lets help this handsome marine to his room..." Cleeve said as he stood up.

"Right with you," Otis said and stood up also.

Holding me by my arms they walked me to the elevators. When the elevator arrived the three of us stepped into it and the doors closed. Cleeve pressed the number fourteen button and the elevator began its ascent.

"When we get to your room we'll call room service and have them bring up a few bottles of scotch for you boy." Cleeve said to me.

"Oh no, I don't think that would be a good idea..." I said my vision blurring.

Then, I had the strangest feeling that Cleeve was kissing me on the mouth. It seemed as though he had wrapped his big arms around me and was forcing his tongue down my throat.

"Ohhh man…" I moaned as my head spun.

Then, I saw Otis' smiling face looking at me and I could have sworn he was kissing me too. When the elevator reached the fourteenth floor the doors opened and we stepped out together, Cleeve and Otis still holding me by my arms. I noticed that my hat was still under my arm. I hadn't dropped it. When we got to my room Otis stuck his hand into the pockets of my uniform jacket, looking for my room key.

"H-hey what're you doin'?" I asked him as Cleeve held me balanced by my arms.

"Just doin' our duty for one of America's best…" Cleeve said, his lips right next to my ear.

As Otis opened the door to my room I felt Cleeve's tongue lap at my ear.

"Hey, what the hell is this?" I asked too late as I realized I was in big trouble.

Cleeve pushed me into my room and Otis closed the door behind us, locking it.

"Shit…*I'm so dizzy…*" I said miserably.

Cleeve pushed me onto my bed and then all I heard was the sound of laughter…

Later…

When I came to a while later I was lying on my bed on my stomach.

"Ohhh man…" I moaned as I woke up, my head feeling like it weighed one hundred pounds.

I lifted my head and was staring at the bed board. It took me a few seconds to realize that my arms were spread wide apart and I was roped at the wrists to the bed board.

"Wh-whass goin' on?" I asked, looking back and forth at the mounds of rope tied tightly around my wrists.

I then realized I was out of uniform. The bastards had stripped me down to just my damned knee length black dress socks.

"What the fuck is going on here???" I yelled, coming out of my stupor.

Suddenly, Cleeve and Otis were standing on the sides of the bed.

"Looks like our boy is awake," Cleeve said, placing a hand on top of my head and stroking my short blond hair. "Feeling okay boy?"

"Y-you two!!" I ranted and managed to pull myself awkwardly to my knees. "You're the two scoundrels I met down in the bar!!"

"Scoundrels!!!" Cleeve and Otis hooted together and laughed hysterically.

"Can't remember the last time I heard that word boy," Cleeve said. "That must be a real down-home Southern expression huh?"

I kneeled there in anger, tugging on the ropes, trying to pull free.

"Fuckin' untie me you bastards!!!" I roared through clenched teeth. "Where's my damned uniform???"

Otis gave me a real hard slap on the ass, moved to the foot of the bed, and grabbed my ankles. With a hard pull he had me lying flat on my stomach again.

"Maybe we should rope his feet to the bed also Cleeve before we do him..." Otis suggested, holding my ankles tight.

"Nah, I like it when they struggle..." Cleeve replied and undid his belt.

"Oh fuck, what---what are you guys thinking about doing to me???" I asked in sudden fear.

"We ain't *thinking* about anything boy." Otis responded and licked the bottom of one of my socked feet long, slow, and hard. "We know what we're going to do to you..."

"Welcome to New York Clifton Davis..." Cleeve said and unbuttoned his jeans.

I lay there and watched helplessly as Cleeve and Otis slowly stripped out of jeans, flannel shirts, construction-boots, and sweat socks. Their bodies were extremely muscular, hairy, and toned. When they shucked off their underpants I saw that they both had enormous dicks...both of them hard, throbbing, and dripping pre cum. Cleeve had the bigger of the two dicks but Otis' was pretty enormous also.

"Oh my word, no, no you guys..." I pleaded, squirming on the bed now.

"Stay still boy!!!" Cleeve yelled and smacked my ass hard. "Now spread those legs boy, wide!!"

"Owwwww!!!" I cried out.

"Oh good God!!!" I cried as Cleeve climbed onto the bed behind me.

"You going to lube him?" Otis asked Cleeve.

"Nah, he's a marine." Cleeve replied with a sneer. "He'll be able to take it..."

"No please don't..." I said softly as Otis pulled one of my legs to the side of the bed. "Oh noooo no..."

Cleeve laid over me on all fours, his lips right by my ear.

"Fuckin' hot lookin' marine you are Clifton Davis..." Cleeve whispered in my ear and gave my earlobe a sharp nip. "However, you never did tell us your rank..."

As Cleeve spoke into my ear I could feel the tip of his dick against my exposed asshole.

"I'm a priv-aaahhhhh!!!" I cried as Cleeve plunged his monster sized hard-on into my asshole.

"Ohhhhrrr yeahhhh!!!" Cleeve gasped as he landed on me. "Fuckin' hot tight hole..."

"Ayyyyy---mmmfff..." I sputtered as Otis shoved one of his foul smelling sweat socks into my mouth, gagging me. "RRRmmfff..."

"Oh yeah Cleeve, give it to him good..." Otis said as he shoved the sock as far as possible into my mouth.

Cleeve rocked up and down on top of me, pumping my hole like crazy, fucking me like mad, and pile driving my virgin asshole.

"Fraggots!!!" I shouted into the gag. "Ruckers!!! RRRRmmfff!!!"

"Oh yeah boy, buck that body for me..." Cleeve crooned. "I love to feel you fight..."

I balled my bound hands into fists and tears of anger and rage flowed from my eyes as I was so brutally raped.

"Ohhhrrr fuck ohhh yeah Otis..." Cleeve said breathlessly. "His hole feels like it's eating my damned dick."

"Fuck him good Cleeve..." Otis said again.

"Fuck, I'm gettin' close already Otis my man!!" Cleeve gasped. "Fuckin' hot guy is going to make me shoot my load...his asshole is so damned tight..."

Cleeve slapped my butt cheeks hard as he continued jack hammering my hole. I felt like I was being stretched like crazy back there. Actually I was.

"Ohhhrrr yeah now Otis, now!!!" Cleeve roared like an animal and shot his giant load into my hole. "Ohhhrr fuck!!!"

"Mmmfff..." I moaned as Cleeve landed on top of me and pumped his load into my hole.

"Ohhh yeah boy, yeahhh..." Cleeve whispered, kissing the back of my neck as he came like crazy.

When he was done he slowly climbed off me and stood on the side of the bed as Otis climbed on behind me.

"MMMfff..." I roared loudly, raising my head up off the bed and looking behind me in disbelief.

The other bastard was about to plunge his big throbbing python into my hole now.

"Oh yeah boy, here I come ready or not..." Otis said and plunged his big dick into my cum drenched hole.

"RRRmmffff!!!" I cried and buried my face in the pillow.

Otis' dick felt as bad as Cleeve's as it hit home and he began fucking me, plowing my hole like a madman in heat. I shook underneath him and when I looked up I saw that Cleeve was sitting on a chair near the bed, sipping scotch from a bottle. No doubt it was the scotch that he and Otis had ordered sent up to my room while I was unconscious.

"Enjoyin' yourself boy?" Cleeve asked me with an evil grin on his face and sipped the scotch.

"RRRmmmffff!!!" I ranted at him, Otis' smelly sweat sock dangling out of my mouth.

The taste of Otis' foot sweat trickled down my throat as he continued fucking me, thrusting in and out of my hole like crazy, slapping my butt cheeks at the same time.

"Ohhh yeahhh fuckin' hot marine you are boy..." Otis crooned, drooling on the back of my neck as he pumped my hole more and more and more. "I'm gettin' close now...ohhhh fuckin' A!!!"

Then, like Cleeve, Otis came in gushes into my poor wounded asshole.

"Ohhhhhrrr yeahhh yeah!!!" Otis roared on top of me, squirting what seemed like gobs upon gobs of cream into my hole.

It felt so hot back there as his cum flooded my hole. His dick made squishing sounds as he pumped me as he came and came. Finally, when he was done his dick slowly slipped out of my hole. He climbed off the bed, took the rancid sock out of my mouth, and sat down on the floor at Cleeve's big naked feet. Cleeve handed Otis the bottle of scotch and Otis took a good swig from it.

"Enjoying your vacation so far boy?" Cleeve asked me mockingly.

"You fucking faggots!!!" I roared at them. "I swear to God I'll kill you both for this!!!"

"First you're goin' to have to get yourself untied boy, and I'll tell you, when Otis and I tie someone up they stay tied up till we decide otherwise." Cleeve said and took a hearty gulp of the scotch.

Otis took one of Cleeve's big feet in his hands and caressed it lovingly. Obviously he was Cleeve's boy. I squirmed miserably on the bed as I felt their cum sliding out of my asshole and onto the sheets.

"Why're you doin' this to me?" I asked them.

Cleeve and Otis looked at each other and laughed at my ridiculous question. It was more than obvious why they were doing this to me. I was a young, hunky marine…just the type that guys like Cleeve and Otis love to work over. When they stopped laughing they stood up and stepped over to the bed.

"Get up on those knees boy." Cleeve said with authority in his voice. "I'm going to lube you for the second round."

"Oh my word no, please no more…" I pleaded.

"Up on those knees I said…" Cleeve said and whacked my ass hard. *"Now!!!"*

Shaking and trembling I pulled myself up to my knees on the bed. Otis proceeded to pull my ass cheeks apart as Cleeve poured some scotch into my gaping and exposed hole.

"Ohhhhh you fuckers…" I swore as my head spun miserably.

In what seemed like the next second Cleeve was on top of me and fucking my hole a second time. His dick felt just as bad as it did the first time he had fucked me. He plowed my hole at what seemed like sixty miles an hour, slapping my ass cheeks hard at the same time. He held the almost empty bottle of scotch in his other hand and took long swigs from it as he went on fucking me.

"Ohhhrrr shit!!!" I said through clenched teeth.

Otis sat on the chair with another bottle of scotch in his hand, his dick long and hard between his legs...no doubt also ready to fuck me a second time.

"Ohhhh yeah fuckin' hot marine..." Cleeve murmured and plowed my hole deeper and deeper.

"Ohhhrrr you bastards!!!" I seethed. "For this I came to New York..."

When Cleeve came the second time he again filled my hole with his juices, rapping my ass cheeks hard. His dick slipped out of my hole, he climbed off the bed, poured the remaining scotch in my sopping wet asshole, and then told Otis to take his second turn at me.

"Ohhhrrr you low lives!!!" I cried as Otis approached the bed.

Cleeve held my ass cheeks apart as Otis poured even more of the scotch into my hole. My head spun and then Otis mounted me and plunged his dick into my hole a second time. A while later the two men were sitting side by side on the couch in my hotel room. I was now lying on my back, tied to the bed in a spread eagle position, and blindfolded.

"You know Otis; we could stay here for the entire week with this hot boy of ours." Cleeve suggested. "I mean, the room is all paid for..."

"No you can't stay here all week!!" I yelled at him. "And I'm not your damned boy!!!"

The two men laughed.

"RRRRR!!!" I roared loudly and tugged on the damned ropes.

"Clifton my boy, you are in no position to be telling us what we can or can't do." Cleeve said and I grimaced miserably behind the blindfold. "Now Otis, I have another suggestion..."

I listened in agony as Cleeve told Otis that they could call friends of theirs on the phone and invite them up to my hotel room for some real fun with a hot marine.

"Fuck fuck fuck..." I whispered angrily.

I felt more stupid than anything else at that moment. My commanding officer and buddies of mine had told me to be wary of overly friendly people in New York. And now, I was in the clutches, and trapped by two of the friendliest people in all of New York City. A little while later Cleeve and Otis poured some of the damned scotch over my bound socked feet and knelt at the foot of the bed licking my socked feet, slurping the scotch off my socks.

"Fucking perverts!!" I yelled angrily. "Licking my damned smelly feet..."

As they licked my feet my dick grew hard between my legs, betraying me...

Then, I felt the scotch poured over my pink nipples and Cleeve and Otis were sucking them...hard...

"Mmmm...nice tits boy..." Cleeve murmured and bit on my nipple that he was working on.

When they'd had enough of my nipples Otis took the blindfold off me and I saw that their damn dicks were hard and throbbing again.

"Ready for round three boy?" Cleeve asked me as he and Otis untied my feet. "This time it's *really* going to fucking hurt..."

"Oh God no, please…" I moaned as Cleeve grabbed my ankles and pushed my legs up and over my head, exposing my asshole.

Holding me in that twisted position by my ankles Cleeve slowly slid his hard dick into my hole.

"Ohhhh yeahhh…" Cleeve moaned in ecstasy. "Warm as a bowl of fresh pudding and tighter than a drum this hole…"

When he plunged in and began thrusting I clenched my teeth as the room started spinning.

"Bastards…" I whispered. *"Fucking low life bastards…"*

Cleeve licked my scotch tasting socks as he fucked me, slightly tickling the bottoms of my feet. When he came he again filled my hole with his hot jizz. Otis wasted no time in scoring a third round fucking my now aching asshole. When they were both done fucking me the third time I lay stretched out again on my bed in a spread eagle position as Otis held my head up by the back of my neck, pouring scotch down my throat. What I didn't swallow dripped out of the sides of my mouth and dripped over my chin and onto my chest.

"Feeling good boy?" Cleeve asked me as Otis fed me the scotch.

"Bastards…" I whispered.

"Hey Otis, lets take him in the bathroom and give his asshole a good cleaning out." Cleeve suggested.

Otis put the bottle of scotch on my night table, looked at Cleeve, and gave him a high five. A few minutes later I was untied from the bed, my socks were off my feet, (I was completely naked now) and Cleeve and Otis held me tightly by my arms as they walked me to the bathroom. I struggled in a drunken stupor in their grasps.

"Fuckin' bastards!!" I roared. "Let go of me and then we'll see just how tough you boys are!!! I'll fuckin' teach you two to fuck a marine's ass…"

In the bathroom they hoisted me into the tub, tied my wrists together in front of me, and tied the slack of the rope to the showerhead. I stood up on my toes as Otis attached a hose to the water faucet.

"Ohhh fuck, no no no…" I groaned miserably.

Moments later the two men were taking turns washing out my asshole. Otis held my ass cheeks apart as Cleeve squirted cold water into my hole and then Cleeve held my ass cheeks apart and Otis would squirt the cold water into my hole.

"Arrrhhhh!!! You fucking bastards!!!" I roared with my back to them.

The two men laughed hysterically as my body quivered and broke out in goose bumps as they washed out my hole with the cold water. My hard dick was pressed up against the cold tile wall and my nipples were erect and hard on my chest. The two men slapped my butt cheeks, prodded my hole with their fingers, (two and three at a time) and went on squirting the icy cold water into my hole. Twice during the ordeal I pissed but the two men didn't seem to notice.

"Man, he has got one of the best asses I have ever seen…or fucked…" Otis commented mockingly.

When they were done and when they were satisfied that my asshole was clean as a whistle they walked me out of the bathroom, my arms strewn across their big shoulders. I was too beat to shit to try anything as they helped me back to the bed. They hoisted me onto my bed and quickly retied me in a spread eagle position. I don't know if I passed out or fell asleep…

The Next Day...

I woke up at eight AM the next morning, still tied to my bed. I could not believe I had slept that way. Cleeve was sound asleep and snoring on the couch. Otis was sleeping soundly on the floor next to the couch. I was no longer drunk...I was ready to teach the two scoundrels a very much needed lesson. But first I would have to get myself loose. Silently I pulled hard on the ropes around my wrists but they were tied too damned tight. I would have to think of something else. I thought of stretching myself upward and trying to untie the knots with my teeth but the ropes around my ankles kept me from even trying that. I would have to think of something else...before the two scoundrels woke up. I looked over at my night table and saw a half-full bottle of scotch. If they fed me any of that first thing in the morning I would be drunk as a skunk after a couple of swigs. Not to mention my stomach was empty. I had not had dinner the night before. What to do to get free...*what a fucked up situation*!!! I tried stretching my fingers toward the knots in the ropes but the knots were way out of my reach. A feeling of utter defeat began to sweep over me. As I lay there utterly helpless Cleeve stopped snoring and began waking up.

"Shit..." I whispered.

He snorted disgustingly as he woke up and smiled maniacally when he looked over at me.

"Man, you sure make it a good morning boy..." he said to me. "Fucking succulent looking marine you are."

Cleeve shook Otis awake and they both came over to the bed. Their hard and throbbing dicks told me I didn't need three guesses to know how they intended to start their day. They untied my feet, pushed my legs up and above me, and proceeded to take turns fucking my hole like crazy. I swore and cursed at them like the marine I am but my words only seemed to drive them on even more. When they couldn't fuck me anymore they (sure enough) made me drink practically all the scotch that was left in the bottle on the night table. As they forced the scotch down my throat I pissed right there on the bed and farted miserably. My stomach was doing flip-flops too. At that moment I wasn't feeling like a real macho kick-ass marine at all. After I was drunk they untied my wrists and walked me to the bathroom for a good shower and another ass cleaning... They roped my wrists above me to the showerhead again, turned on the cold water, and soaped me up everywhere, sticking their fingers deep into my hole.

"Arrrhhghhh!!! You fuckers!!!" I ranted. "Slimy scoundrels..."

My hard dick was again pressed against the cold tile wall. As they cleaned out my hole, squirting cold water into it with that blasted hose I found myself rubbing my boner against the wall.

"Hey Cleeve, he's jerkin' himself off..." Otis commented.

"Let him." Cleeve said. "With what he's been through and with what he's about to go through he deserves it."

I rubbed my boner harder and harder against the tile wall and then I shot a marine sized load of spunk.

"Ohhhrrr yeahhh yeahhh!!!" I roared in agony and ecstasy at the same time, shooting my load all over the wall.

Cleeve and Otis cheered me on wildly, slapping my butt cheeks hard as I came and came, shooting what seemed like gobs of creamy spunk out of my hole.

"Ohhhh..." I moaned.

When I was done they gave my balls a few good pulls, twists, and squeezes. I pissed a long hard stream next, washing my cum off the wall. What was left they ran their fingers through and fed to me. I had no choice but to lick my cum and piss off their fingers.

After they were done washing me down they brought me out of the bathroom and again tied me to my bed on my stomach, my wrists roped tightly to the bed board.

"Some of our buddies should be here real soon..." Cleeve said as he shoved one of my socks from the day before into my mouth. "And boy oh boy are they in for a real treat..."

"RRRRmmmfff!!!" I sputtered and thrashed wildly on the bed, the taste of my own foot stink on my day old sock mixed with scotch assaulting my taste-buds and dripping down my throat.

And sure enough, about ten minutes later there was a knock on my hotel room door. Otis opened the door and six guys came into my room, all of them big burly looking fuckers. At the sight of me they oooed and ahhhed like crazy.

"Whoa!!! Fuckin' hot lookin' marine you nailed guys." one of them said.

"Let me at that guy." another one of them said gleefully.

"What a sweet lookin' ass he has..." still another one of them said.

I watched as they all quickly stripped naked. Damn, from the sizes of their dicks my ass was about to be plowed more than a farm field. The first guy who was naked jumped on the bed behind me, pulled me up to my knees, spread my ass cheeks apart, and plunged his giant boner into my hole.

"RRRmmmfff..." I roared miserably.

"Good thing you gagged him Cleeve." Otis said with a grin on his face.

"Yeah..." Cleeve agreed.

While the first guy was fucking me two of the other guys were licking my feet while the rest of them were all reaching for my marine chest, taking turns squeezing my nipples and pecs.

"Fruckers…" I moaned into my sock gag.

The first guy came in gushes into my hole and then another guy took his place.

"Ohhhh yeahhh goin' to fuck you good and hard you hot marine…" the next guy said as he positioned himself behind me.

It went on like that for what seemed like hours. A few of the guys took second and third turns fucking my poor hole and even Cleeve and Otis took another turn each at my hole.

"Damn, by the time we're all done his hole is goin' to be mince meat…" I heard one of the bastards say.

Then, when they all couldn't fuck me anymore they turned me over onto my back and tied me at the wrists and ankles in a spread eagle position. They were all on me like white on rice, licking, sucking, biting, and squeezing my nipples, licking my feet and balls, and even stroking my dick. They forced me to cum two times, making me piss all over myself in between my jizz shots. They delighted in making me drink more of the scotch and by the time they were all done with me I was a sweaty stinking mess of a marine. I passed out for sure because when I opened my eyes they were all gone… including Cleeve and Otis. I was lying on my bed on my back, completely untied. My sock was out of my mouth and on the bed next to me. As I slowly sat up (shaking and trembling) it felt as if a dick was still rammed far up my ass. Sitting there I realized that there was a dick up my ass. Actually, the scoundrels had left a big old dildo stuck in my asshole. Slowly, I pulled on it, fucking myself this time. As I thrust the dildo in and out of my hole my dick grew hard between my legs.

"Oh my word…" I whispered. "What have they made of me???"

I jerked myself off and came in gushes as I fucked my hole more and more with the dildo. When I was done gushing I pulled the thing completely out but I knew it wouldn't be long before I would want it again and again and again… I walked on wobbly feet to the bathroom and took a long and warm shower.

"Ahhhh…warm water feels fucking great…" I said to myself as the water cascaded over my body.

I washed out my hole thoroughly, wondering if I was doing so to get the feel of the scoundrels off me or because it felt so damned good as I did it. After I was done showering I realized I was starving. I dried off, pulled on a pair of white cotton boxer shorts and a pair of knee length black socks and called room service. I ordered a hearty breakfast and lots of coffee. Within fifteen minutes there was a knock at my door.

"Who is it?" I called out as I walked over to the door in just my socks and boxers.

"Room service…" a voice replied.

I opened the door and two handsome bellboys wheeled my breakfast in. As I closed the door they looked me over and smiled at me. I smiled right back. Seconds later my boxers were around my ankles and I stood with my legs spread as one of the bellboys fucked my hole and the other one chowed down on my nipples… As I said earlier, this should never happen to another marine…

About the Author

Christopher Trevor

Christopher Trevor was born in July 1963 and grew up in New York City. As soon as he was old enough to know how he began writing fiction and has been writing gay erotic/fetish stories for the past ten to twelve years at this point. He became an avid reader as well from the time he knew how and reads everything from fiction, to non-fiction to biographies of interesting and unusual people, people who have made a difference or who have paved the way for others. Christopher attributes his writing artistic inspiration to artists such as Etienne, Tom of  Finland, Tagame, The Hun, and most notably Joe T, who Christopher has had the pleasure of speaking with and even meeting over the last few years. Christopher states, "Joe T encouraged me to write about my fetish because I was embarrassed about it at the time. Joe T said that when we are embarrassed about something that makes it even more enticing somehow." Christopher totally agreed and never stopped writing in this genre. Erotic writers who inspired Christopher Trevor were: Tom Shaw (author of "That Day at the Quarry), C.S. White (author of Big Sur), Larry Townsend (author of countless erotic novels), and Mason Powell (author of the classic story "The Brig.")

Christopher discovered that not only did he enjoy writing erotic tales but that after his first bondage experience he had a genuine flair for it. Writing to erotic oriented magazines about his first bondage experience truly opened the floodgates for Christopher where this style of writing is concerned. Christopher thanks the handsome and muscular "Greg" for that experience way back in time. Christopher took "Creative Writing" courses every semester during his high school years and while other friends of his stopped writing what they loved to write about as time went on Christopher never let a day go by when he didn't write something... "I feel that if I don't write every day I will die," Christopher has said many times over.

Foot fetish stories and all things related; spanking fetish, erotic shaving, muscle bondage, tickle torture, and hardcore stories are just a few of the areas of gay eroticism that Christopher enjoys writing about and inspiring in others as well. As one internet buddy said to Christopher where the black socks fetish is concerned, "Until I started talking with you I never gave a thought to my socks when I got dressed for work in the morning. Now when I pull my dress socks on every morning I get a chill up my spine."

Christopher is proud of the erotic effect he has on people...

Christopher Trevor is also the author of:

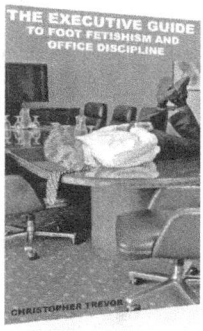  

  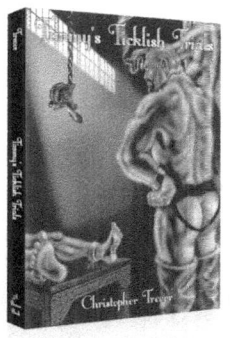

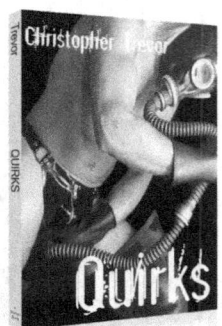

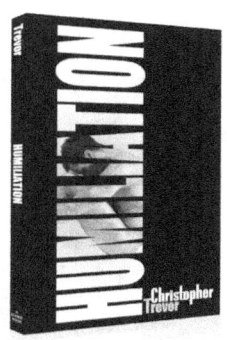